Stanley is almost fifty. He hates his job, has an overbearing mother, and is in a failed relationship. Then he meets Asher, the man of his dreams, literally in his dreams.

Asher is young, captivating, and confident about his future—everything Stanley is not. So, Asher gives Stan a gift. The chance to be an extra five years younger each time they meet.

Some of their adventures are whimsical. A few are challenging. Others are totally surreal. All are designed to bring Stan closer to the moment his joyful childhood turned to tears.

But when they fall in love, Stan knows he can't live in Asher's dreamworld. Yet he is haunted by Asher's invitation to "slip into eternal sleep."

I0583996

THE MIDNIGHT
MAN

Kevin Klehr

A NineStar Press Publication

www.ninestarpress.com

The Midnight Man

Printed in the USA

ISBN: 978-1-64890-358-8

First Edition, August, 2021

Also available in eBook, ISBN: 978-1-64890-357-1

CONTENT WARNING:
This book contains sexual content, which may only be suitable for mature readers. Depictions of cheating, multiple partners, drug use, assault, trauma (past), and homophobic slurs.

Chapter One

Laid

Stanley gazed into the fridge as he waited for his partner, Francesco, and their conquest for the night to stop smooching at the front door and come inside.

He checked for eggs and milk. He was thankful there were chives in a container so breakfast for their guest could be a tad more exotic. But he'd have to go easy on the toast as there were only three slices of sourdough left, and he didn't want to open the boring old multigrain.

He closed his eyes to recall the night. Their plaything was licking his lips with just the right amount of tongue when he propositioned Francesco at the nightclub. He hadn't even noticed Stanley.

But if the couple didn't respond to the young man's request, he'd move on to the next potentials and Stanley and Francesco would have to choose between those altered by alcohol or happy pills. And Stanley knew those sins outstayed their welcome like bad wallpaper. Fortunately, tonight's pickup was only slightly wired.

Francesco stumbled in the living room, trying to make martinis. Their boy was giggling like a pre-schooler who'd heard a limerick. But the disco laden images of earlier that night were still haunting Stanley.

Francesco's workmate, Graham, had joined them with his partner, Tony. Stanley recalled the look Tony gave them when they said goodnight. As if their hookup, who wrapped his arms around Stanley and Francesco, was the victim in some lost midlife scenario reminiscent of anxious porn. Yet Graham and Tony were only ten years older than Stanley and Francesco's toy for the night. Surely Tony would be more open-minded.

"Dinky, the martinis are ready."

Stanley frowned at hearing his nickname. It was his curtain call to re-enter this flawed three-character play.

"Elijah can't believe you're fifty soon," Francesco said, handing Stan his cocktail.

"You look so good." The lad gazed wide-eyed for more time than naturally required. "Your hair's thinning a little, but I know guys half your age who are seriously bald."

"See, Dinky. Even Elijah thinks you're handsome for your age."

"Thank you," Stanley mumbled. He sat on the edge of the armrest of the large sofa.

Elijah sat with his legs stretched out, enjoying the comfort of their recliner as if it was his own. He grinned at Francesco like a patient kid waiting too long for dessert.

"I hope you like scrambled eggs," Stanley said.

"Say what?" Elijah snickered.

"You said you were staying for breakfast," Stan replied. "You said so on the ride home."

"Oh no." Elijah looked horrified, as if dessert were cancelled. "You're taking me out for breakfast."

"He wants to be paraded," said Francesco.

"Like a gold medal." Stanley tried his best not to roll his eyes.

"So, what made you choose *us* tonight?" Francesco asked.

"You're an established couple," Elijah replied. "You know your shit. And you've dealt with your shit. Older men are so much more fun." He turned to Stanley. "Most times I go out, I pick up an older couple."

Stanley couldn't help thinking how rehearsed Elijah sounded. "Has that strategy always worked?"

"Of course."

"Really?"

Elijah stared blankly at Stanley. "Yeah, except when one guy is more uptight than the other."

"I think we should get down to business." Francesco laughed. "We're all here for the same thing."

"Of course." Elijah didn't break eye contact with Stanley.

"Absolutely," Stanley replied.

"Can I talk to you for a moment, Dinky?"

Francesco strolled past Stanley, who reluctantly followed him into their bedroom.

"Think of it as an early birthday gift. A way to recapture your youth."

"Franky, I don't trust him."

"We're having sex with him. We're not signing a business contract with him."

"He has attitude."

"He's on drugs. And you know the drugs today. They're not chill pills like in our day. Please, Dinky, do this for *me*."

"Why do you want this so badly?"

Francesco exhaled and sat on the edge of the bed. "Dinky, it's a bit of fun, for goodness' sake. Don't overthink it. Joke with the guy. I'm sure you and Joel will have a good time."

"Elijah."

"What?"

"His name is Elijah. You said his name ten minutes ago when you told me he can't believe I'm nearly fifty."

"Where did I get Joel from?"

"He was last week's guy. You remember. Intense, but nice."

"Oh yeah. He lived with his mother. Some tragic story about his father leaving."

"That's the one. He had a bent dick. It was like sucking a banana sideways."

Francesco chuckled. "His knob kept grazing against my back teeth. How I didn't scratch him I'll never know. It's probably an occupational hazard."

Stanley smirked.

"There, Dinky. That's better. You light up when you smile. Elijah hasn't seen that side of you tonight. You'll win him over. You'll see." Francesco stood. "What's on your mind?"

Stanley didn't answer. The stark tree, his favourite outside the bedroom window, took his attention. He'd study it like an ink blot test, seeing what its knots and patterns reminded him of, whenever he couldn't express himself. Or, whenever he knew expressing himself was a waste of time with Francesco.

"You're thinking about something you're not telling me."

"It's okay. It's nothing."

Francesco reached for the top drawer next to his bed. Inside a small ornamental tin was his dope stash. Next to it were his papers. He rolled a joint.

"Dinky, he's here now, waiting for us. Let's have fun."

Francesco was about to light the joint, but Stanley shook his head. Instead, he raised his martini and Stanley reluctantly clinked his glass. Elijah sauntered in, naked.

"This is my ice breaker," the lad said. "When my hookups leave me alone for too long, I..."

Elijah sank into their antique armchair and spread out so the couple could scrutinise his masculinity. It was already at half-mast. Francesco offered a puff, but Elijah waved it away. Stanley took it and drew on it anxiously like a prisoner facing a firing squad.

He passed the joint to Francesco, but he handed it back, believing Stan needed it more than he did. Another puff reduced Stan's angst.

"Why don't you take your clothes off?" Elijah asked.

Francesco loosened his belt and unzipped his jeans. He could smell youth in front of him, and in that mystical deodorised scent, he felt the stirrings of his own younger self. He took a swig of his martini and placed it on their teak drawers. This was foremost, his preferred drug of denial.

Stanley stood next to the chair, steadily undoing the buttons on the striped shirt that hung over his waist. Then he stopped.

Elijah played with his own nipple. *You want me, and you're not in control!*

Francesco willingly reached for the lad's other nipple.

Stanley watched, gradually moving behind the chair. *Why am I here?* The joint was still smouldering, so he took another hit. Many unresolved feelings accompanied the smoke into his lungs. Shame. Despair. Loneliness. The last was the hardest to digest. It sailed deeper than his breath. He closed his eyes.

"Earn it," Francesco growled at Elijah.

A boyish grunt followed a manly groan. This pattern seesawed until one could not be distinguished from the other. A lad learning from his elder how to moan like an adult.

A hand reached for Stanley, unzipping him, and in his daze he moved forward. A mouth was tasting him below. But Stan stayed distant in his mind. His troubled emotions had to be kept at bay. He numbed himself of all the things he'd left unsaid as he let the lad pleasure him. Tears of sorrow were passed off as tears of delight.

Stan pictured a bathtub. Bubbles floated, bursting on the tiles. Francesco was with him, younger, kissing Stanley amid the foam. A playful ruffle of hair. A finger tracing its way to Stan's toes. A gentle caress to Stanley's rosy tip.

His stomach churned. This was the first signal of the end of this ordeal. His detached manhood whirled on a parallel plain. Soon he'd be streaming what was expected of him—an action pure and direct.

White lines christened Elijah. His chest claimed evidence of another man's satisfaction.

Francesco peered at his partner. One hand still clutched their guest while the other hand brought the last drop of his martini to his lips. With a poker face he declared, "Happy premature birthday, Stan."

"Do you remember his name?" Graham asked.

"Believe it or not, I do," Francesco replied.

A man came into the box office.

"I'll deal with this one, Frank. But I want all the sordid details when I'm done."

Graham looked through the tray of tickets for tonight's performance. It was a period piece set in an Ancient Arabic kingdom.

"It's quite a show," he said to the theatregoer. "It's our company's most expensive production. When you see the stage design, you'll think you're at the opera. What did you say your name was? Oh, no, don't worry. I've found you. Peters. Geoffrey Peters. Two tickets in row D."

Graham checked the date to be sure before he handed them over as Francesco often placed tickets in the wrong tray—*6 March 2011*. Correct.

Geoffrey checked them before mentioning how much he treasured shows that were grand. He then skipped away with a redheaded man, prepared for a night of prestigious entertainment.

"Any camper and he'd fart glitter," Francesco said.

"I'd do him."

"That could mean two things, and if it's the second thing I'm thinking of, you'd have a lot to explain to Tony when he sees your glittering cock."

The pair laughed as more people arrived for the show. When the first act began, Graham leaned forward in anticipation for Francesco's bedroom confessions.

"He had a tattoo. Do all kids his age have a tattoo?"

"Tony's got a tattoo."

"What of?" Now Francesco leaned forward.

"He has a dragon soaring in front of a kite. But that's not important. What was this guy like?"

"A bit bratty. He wanted breakfast in a café the next morning."

"Why was that a problem?"

"I prefer the old-fashioned way. A cup of coffee and scrambled eggs on toast, all created in the comfort of your own kitchen. It's called entertaining a guest."

"You don't mind being seen in public with a flirtatious guy."

Francesco smirked. "Am I that easy to read?"

"If you could have a dozen shirtless men feeding you grapes in the middle of the city, you'd still ask passers-by to snap your picture just to make sure they'd notice. Besides, Frank, you can't cook."

"True. But I make a wicked martini."

A latecomer charged into the box office. "Your name?" Francesco asked. She replied and was promptly handed her ticket before she raced to the theatre door.

"What should we do for Stan's birthday?" Graham asked.

"He doesn't want a party."

"That doesn't mean we shouldn't throw him one."

"I've been thinking about it. A surprise party in our home. Several carnival themed strippers. Enough party pills to induce a coronary. And a shirtless bartender who makes wicked margaritas."

"Frank, think for a minute. Aren't you forgetting something?"

"What?"

"This is Stanley's birthday. Not yours."

Chapter Two

Midnight

"Sex would be nice," Stanley said.

It was just after eleven at night when Francesco came home from his shift at the theatre. His partner was waiting, wearing nothing but a robe.

"Why did you get out of bed?" Francesco asked.

"I've already told you." Stanley attempted a sly grin. "It's time for love, my love."

Francesco forced a smile. "You are such a beautiful man, Stanley, but it's been a long night."

"And I know you, Franky. You'll toss and turn because you can't sleep, and I have just the antidote for insomnia." He flashed his cock.

"Didn't you get enough love over the weekend?"

"Yeah, but threesomes are a poor substitute to when it's just *us* making love."

"Hmm."

Francesco made his way to the kitchen and in no time had a saucepan of milk, enough for two cups, on the stove. Stanley followed, slipped his robe off, and stood near the fridge with a pensive look.

But Francesco shut his tired eyes, hoping to block out the world. "Don't get too close, Dinky. I might accidentally burn you."

Stanley sighed. "Okay, Franky. I get it. You need sleep."

His partner poured the warm milk. They drank in silence. Stanley pondered Francesco's tone when he used his nickname, Dinky. It was invented by Francesco early in their relationship, but Stanley remembered the gorgeous smile that came with the word whenever it was uttered. These days it was said as if a father was trying to escape spending time with his kid so he could run off to his mistress. *Dinky, I'm busy. Haven't you got friends your own age to play with?*

It had been a while since Francesco felt guilty fobbing off Stanley's advances. They still had sex, but not as often as either had hoped, and never without a third. *Should we talk about this?* Francesco thought. *Why can't we both be in the mood at the same time?* But he didn't know how to bring up the conversation, and with his partner drinking milk in the nude, it was not a tactical moment.

"Time for bed, I guess," Stanley said.

"Tomorrow night, Dinky. Let's make love tomorrow night."

★

The alarm clock ticked loudly at the side of their bed, and while Francesco snored like a buzz saw clearing a rain forest, Stanley lay awake. It wasn't his partner who was the cause of his insomnia for Stanley could doze through the wildest storm. In fact, Stanley was sound asleep only ten minutes prior until he thought he heard someone whisper in his ear.

The arms of his alarm clock inched their way toward the number twelve. He sat up and, shortly after, stood and took his dressing gown from the bed post. He remembered hearing the word "eternal" in the sentence that was murmured to him, but the rest of the phrase was hazy.

Numerous cats meowed in unison. Stanley was unnerved. He strode to the living room and peeked through the curtain. Several feline gangs gathered on the front lawn. An eerie wind shook the trees as the cats strolled to the centre of the garden.

Stanley studied the sky. Not a star in sight. Nor was there a cloud above, so the lack of any sign of the universe made no sense. He pondered the end of humanity before concerning himself with his morbid train of thought. The voice whispered again, and Stanley instantly felt drowsy. He sauntered back to the bedroom and fell on top of the sheets.

In his slumber, his dreams began, and in this personal movie he sat at a small round table in a circular room. A crimson curtain wrapped itself around the space.

A crisp white tablecloth fell just above his knees and embossed on a shiny gold card in the middle of his table were the words: RESERVED. THE MIDNIGHT MAN.

There were other tables too. All with the same small card and all with either a mature-aged man or woman sitting at them. The only difference was, each of these people were dining and chatting with a younger male companion.

He noted the dress code. Every man, young or old, sported a dinner suit. Stanley also wore one. Each lady was adorned in a stylish black dress.

"Excuse me, sir." Stanley looked up. A tall waiter with a quaint moustache addressed him. "I'm sorry to say your Midnight Man is running late."

"Okay," he replied, mumbling.

With time to spare, Stanley picked up the card. He gazed at it, giving the appearance it aroused his curiosity, but he was actually eavesdropping. He eased back in his chair to listen to the woman who was sitting behind him.

"I feel useless in my job. It's like I'm invisible. I drag myself in day after day as my colleagues keep getting promoted. Even the ones who haven't been there as long as I have rise up that ladder." She sniffled. Her dinner companion pulled out a handkerchief. She took it but was too embarrassed to blow her nose. "Thank you, Declan. I'm sorry to splurge like this."

Her office sounds like mine, Stanley thought.

Declan got up and gently caressed her arm. "There's no shame in being upset," he said. "That's why I'm here. Think of me as your priest. Confide in me. And just like a man of god, I'm here to make sure all pain goes away."

"Interesting conversation?" This questioning voice startled Stanley, but boy, was it sexy. Its honey-rich timbre could invite you to a murder and you'd stay under its spell until the moment the knife was placed in your hand. Stanley looked up to see whose voice it was.

A young man stood with hands in his trouser pockets. His smile sent Stan's thoughts spinning. Stan knew a genuine grin and this lad had no hidden agendas lurking behind his cordial manner. Stanley was convinced of it.

He measured up to all the best-looking groomsmen Stanley had admired at the various weddings he'd attended. Most of the time it was the best man Stan fancied, especially if they were still playing the field. He'd stare at them wishing to be swept off his feet and carried down the aisle.

This Midnight Man had a crew cut. It's a cliché to say it was the preferred style of boy next door types, but for Stan, it sealed the deal. Something classic. Something captivating. Something familiar enough to help him not feel old.

"I'm Asher." He held out his hand. Stanley took it, holding onto it until Asher seated himself at the table.

"You're beautiful," Stanley heard himself saying. "Sorry, I don't mean to be forward. It's just that…" He covered his mouth momentarily. "How old are you?"

"Twenty-one."

"You're the perfect age."

"What for? For you?" Asher smirked with bedroom confidence.

"No. No. I didn't mean it like that. You're my perfect *age*. No. I'm not making myself clear, am I?"

Asher reached across the table and tenderly stroked Stanley's wrists.

"It's just…" Stan continued. "It's just that twenty-one was the last age I was truly happy. The world was mine and everyone around me seemed alive!" His eyes watered. "Sorry. These are the ramblings of someone staring at fifty."

"I've never had that effect on anyone before. Please talk. You're interesting."

"Interesting? You hardly know me."

"I know this much about you. I know you have a partner, but you need to meet me. I know that somewhere buried inside the man looking at me is confidence waiting to be freed from captivity. I know that if I can make your face light up, we'll all see how devilishly cute you are."

"I wish the last part was true. You're teasing me, Ash."

"I'm intrigued. Why was twenty-one your last happy year?"

"I don't know. I remember every year leading up to my twenty-first. All of them were magic. My mum took me everywhere and I learned to be social at an early age. But I don't want to bore you with my childhood memories."

"Do I look bored?" Asher wiggled an eyebrow.

"No. You look cheeky." Stanley gasped. "Here I am, an old man drooling over someone less than half my age. I'm sorry."

"Hey, it's your dream. Anything could happen." He wiggled his eyebrow once more. "Now, you were talking about your twenty-one-year-old self."

"No, this is silly." Stanley glanced at the other young men in this scene. "I don't meet guys in my dreams."

"Do you want to sleep with me?"

"I didn't say that."

"But it was on your mind." Asher grinned to himself. "Stan, I want to know what type of year I'm about to have. I'm *your* ideal age—twenty-one. Tell me about your twenty-first year. I have a lot to learn."

"That's easy. Every part of the jigsaw was in place when I was twenty-one. I was cocksure, dancing night after night with no cares. My job was easy, though at times demanding, but I had it under control. Plus, I had cash to burn, so it was a great time to be alive."

"Don't stop, Stan. I want to hear more. I want all the details. Did you fall for anyone that year?"

"I experienced all my heartbreak before twenty-one. And I broke a heart or two. That made me determined to stay single until the right guy came along."

Stanley paused, lost in thought.

"Are you hungry?" Asher asked. "Should I ask the waiter for the menu? I'm looking forward to sitting here and listening to your tales."

"Strangely, I don't have an appetite."

"Me neither." They were the only people in the room now. "Maybe your dream needs a change of pace." Asher stood. "Follow me to enchantment, or something close to it."

Stanley did as he was told. Through the crimson curtain was an opening. As they ventured through the darkness on the other side, music broke through the silence. The floor shook with each beat. The murmur of a crowd brought back many memories for Stanley, and as the laser lights flashed random colour into the void, the crowd became visible. Everyone was Asher's age. Everyone was male. Stanley reached for Asher's hand to lead him through this curious scene. They were both dressed differently.

Stanley wore a waistcoat adorned with tiny roses, buttoned tight to expose his chest. Asher wore a blue T-shirt as he strode toward the DJ. Stan looked down at a smiling quarter moon, the oversized design on his belt buckle. He stomped his foot. His shoes were sturdy, leather and unmistakably British.

It's perfect in every way, he thought. So perfect in fact, he was waiting for the ecstasy to kick in. He worked his way back to Asher.

"Why are you called the Midnight Man?" he yelled over the house tune.

"We're all Midnight Men," Asher called back. "Everyone dining with your generation in that restaurant was a Midnight Man."

"But what does it mean?"

"It's the time I entered your life—midnight." His playful grin returned.

"You're not telling me much."

"You didn't tell me much about your life either."

"I opened up."

"Just the outline. Not the details." Asher stopped where they were and danced. "Are you always this cautious?"

"Yes. Even with people I trust." As Stanley said the last word, he could feel a change.

First, the music. It sounded hollow, as if someone had played around with an equaliser and got it all wrong. Then, like a jet engine, it soared.

Next, awareness of his own lanky shape was replaced by a oneness with everyone in that huge hall. There were no creaky joints or sagging skin. Decades disappeared. A sense of love so overwhelming consumed him. And in this micro moment, Asher was arguably the most bewitching guy Stanley had ever met in the decades he walked the earth.

Then it hit full charge. The need to dance! The want to take off his waistcoat and sense the sweat, the pleasure, and the energy that took control. He was lost in sensation. He was lost in thoughts that highlighted every positive thing about himself. He hadn't felt this for a very long time.

And Asher was part of this charge, the best part. A boy at the start of the finest years of his life. Young enough to be sought after and brave enough to seek love from those who'll fall under his spell.

The guys nearby were eyeing Stanley. One, with a superhero logo painted on his muscular torso, slid his own hand down past his navel and into his shorts. He seemed familiar. Stanley met him in his early adult years. A face faded by memory coming back to relive his days of confidence.

But beside this tool of seduction was another face lost in time. A lover Stanley recalled for his kindness at a time when he was finding himself. This guy waved at Stanley. The gesture was returned with an air kiss.

Coming toward them was a guy who sported small mirror tiles on his shoulders, as if he was a walking disco ball. He had similarly mirrored shorts. And he also held a mirror.

To Stanley, this guy wore the face of a human hiding his hurt. Someone wishing others would understand his sadness, yet too polite to talk about his feelings, or cry until there were no more tears. A feeling too familiar.

Stanley raised his arms and shook his butt, encouraging Mirror Ball Man to find his bliss. For a moment, the guy laughed. A door was open, ready for pain to be released. He swung his hips, making his way toward Stanley, so Stanley raised his arms higher to transmit love in all directions. Then the guy held his mirror to Stanley's face.

There it was. There was no denying it. Stanley was not twenty-one again. He was nearly fifty. A man in need of maturity.

"What is it?" Asher asked.

Mirror Ball Man was nowhere to be seen.

"I'm not meant to be here."

Stanley sat startled as he found himself opposite Asher back at the restaurant. Both were wearing suits again.

"So, tell me, Stan, where are you meant to be?"

Chapter Three

Flowers

"This place looks like a funeral parlour. And it smells like one too."

Francesco came home from the matinee shift at the theatre and was confronted by a living room full of flowers. There were classic red roses in a vase on a side table, Australian natives on the dining table and a humongous white bouquet covering the surface of the coffee table. And while he appreciated Stanley's taste in florals, he felt a stress headache coming along.

He marched up to Stanley and stared straight into his eyes. "Why are you home at quarter past four in the afternoon?"

"I took the afternoon off," Stanley replied.

"Why?"

"I needed alone time to think."

"What about, for goodness' sake?"

"About my life."

"Really? And what conclusions did you come to, Dinky?"

"My life isn't right."

"And that's why you bought all these flowers?"

"Yeah, but my life still isn't right."

Francesco staggered to an armchair and then sank into it trying not to feel agitated.

"How much did you spend on these flowers?"

"Five hundred."

Francesco shot straight back up. "Are you crazy?"

"Hear me out, Franky. I needed a romantic gesture, so I gave myself one."

"Yes, a five-hundred-dollar gesture!" Francesco rubbed his forehead. "Gees Louise. I know we haven't had sex alone in a while, but it was a joint decision to experiment."

"Franky, to be honest I don't know why I spent so much." He picked one of the roses from its vase and took in its odour. Its fresh scent eased him. "Look at our place. It's colourful and beautiful. All the things that life should be."

Francesco's tongue froze. A sense of dread weighed on his heart. *What's going on?* He strolled to the bar, attempting to calm himself.

"Would you like a martini, Dinky?"

"I can't. It's Tuesday."

"Of course. It's 'dinner at your mum's' night. Your weekly catch-up to bitch about me." Francesco tried to laugh at his own joke. "It's still early. One drink now won't affect how you drive in a couple of hours."

"Mum knows I'm home, so she's asked me over early."

"All right."

Francesco poured vermouth into the metal shaker, followed by a handful of ice. As he reached for the gin, he watched Stanley pick up a vase of tulips, inspect them, and place them down again. Stanley continued inhaling the collection, almost dancing around each bouquet like Adam exploring the Garden of Eden. Francesco's hand shook a little as he reached for a glass, so he stopped for a moment and considered his own feelings about his partner's weird behaviour. Unnerved. Scared. *Has dementia set in?*

Francesco considered their seven years together knowing Stanley had never acted like this. So, there was no frame of reference that could throw light on this deranged whimsy.

"Dinky, let's have sex before you see your mother."

"Why?"

"It's what you want, isn't it?" Francesco forced a grin. Stanley scowled. "Or we can just lie in bed, caress, and talk."

"Franky, we have a room full of flowers. Go online. Let's have a sexual adventure and show off our love nest."

Stan's tone is different, Francesco thought. *He sounds like a naive heroine in a romance novella.*

"Who would you like to have sex with?" Francesco asked, cautiously.

"A couple."

"A couple?"

"Yes. And not too young."

"But you like younger men, Dinky."

"But we're old men, Franky. We should act out our fantasies with another established couple."

"If that's what you want, I have an idea." Francesco wrangled up a genuine smile. "Our 'love nest' will be ready for action tomorrow night."

★

Adelaide made sure there wouldn't be a hair out of place when her son, Stanley, was due to arrive at her high-rise. Half a can of hairspray was used to make certain each follicle obeyed like a loyal soldier. She applied the same green eye shadow and shade of pink lipstick she had used for the last fifty years. And she chose a sensible yet stylish brown dress and white pearls as her outfit for the evening.

Stanley could smell the roast as he entered. Tonight, it was beef. He couldn't recall if it was lamb or chicken the week before, as there was no predetermined order to which livestock would give up mortality for the dinner plate. One roast meal after another, over so many years, made each one seem the same. But Stanley embraced this sense of familiarity.

To please his mother, he wore a tie tonight.

"You seem happier than usual, Stanley."

"Life's good," he replied.

He wandered into her spacious apartment. The moonlight skipped on the ripples of the expansive ocean. *Nature at its finest*, Stanley thought as he looked through the giant window in her dining room. Then he inspected the blue tablecloth matched with the gold-rimmed white china his mother recently added to her extensive dinnerware collection.

Adelaide lived for Tuesday night meals with her son. Her chance to feel she had family. This north-side flat was the only one she hadn't rented out, and she made sure she was always here for his visits and not at the home he was raised in. Stanley preferred it this way.

The cleaner had done a sterling job, as always, in keeping all Adelaide's white furniture spotless. The vanilla theme was extended to the carpet, the kitchen floorboards and cabinetry, and her very expensive television set.

Adelaide poured two glasses of sherry.

"Why are you in such fine spirits?" she asked. "Has Francesco finally ended his secret affair?"

"Mother! I don't know where you get that idea from."

"Just a hunch. And I'm never wrong about my hunches. Although I'm still not sure what you're doing with that man."

"Mother, I don't need to hear it again."

"I raised you to do better. And it's still early enough to leave. Move in here for a while until you get sorted out."

"And no matter who I fall in love with they won't be good enough for you. You wouldn't leave Samuel alone, and he was worthy of your class!"

"*Our* class, Stanley. It's *our class*."

"Do we need to have this conversation again?"

"But darling—"

"No, I'm serious. Mum, it got old six years ago. I love Franky and he loves me—"

"Even in this seven-year itch period?"

"We work through it our own way."

"Yes, by turning a blind eye to Francesco's adultery."

"Mother!"

"Okay, I'll shut up about it."

"I wouldn't mind if you had proof but all you have is a hunch. And yes, before you repeat yourself, I know you had that same hunch before Dad ran off, but seriously, I think I'd have that hunch, too, if Franky was in love with someone else."

"You quivered."

"I what?"

"You quivered halfway through your sentence. You have that *same* hunch."

"Oh, Mother." Stanley made his way to the sherry bottle and topped both their glasses. "Let's talk about something else."

The oven timer chimed.

"You'll be pleased with tonight's dinner," Adelaide declared. "I've dipped the carrots in honey."

She reached for her apron and oven mitts, both in snow white. Erroneous colour, even down to the accessories, was never an option in this apartment.

As the oven door opened, the tempting odour of slow roasted beef brought a childlike grin to Stanley's face.

"You've used sage." He inhaled. "How come you stopped baking?" He breathed the scent in further.

"I'm baking now. What are you talking about?"

"You haven't used sage for a very long time. You used to roast often."

"I make a roast for you each week. You're talking nonsense, Stanley."

"And you used to make a roast each week when I was young. But you stopped."

"I stopped?"

"Yes. When I hit my adult years, you stopped roasting succulent dinners with sage. You heated frozen foods instead."

"I make roasts for you now."

"But why did you stop?"

Her head slumped, but when she became aware of herself, she forced a smile and turned to Stanley.

"I lost interest in roasting."

"You lost interest in a lot of things. Was it because you got that hunch about Dad?"

"Perhaps."

"No. Come to think of it, *you* changed before Dad left. Mum, you opened the world to me when I was a kid. Theatre. Arty cinema. Galleries. We saw every exhibition and every must-see movie up until I was twenty-one. What made you change?"

"You had more on your mind at twenty-one than culture. You had your eye on every available boy, and some not so available."

"Was Dad playing around before his affair?"

Adelaide slammed the oven door shut and then composed herself as if nothing happened.

"Let's make a deal, Stanley. I won't talk about your love choices if you stop talking about mine."

Chapter Four

Proposition

"What a great surprise!" Stanley entered his home after another mind-numbing day at the office.

"*You're* surprised?" Graham replied. "What do you think we said when we saw all these flowers?"

Francesco was already sharing martinis with Tony and Graham and had one waiting for his partner on the tiny space left on the end of the coffee table that wasn't taken up by a huge floral display.

"What's the occasion?" Tony asked.

"Do you mean for tonight's invitation, or for all the flowers?" Francesco asked.

"Both," Graham replied.

"The flowers were my impulse buy," Stanley confessed. "But looking at them now, I guess I went overboard."

"They lighten the place," Francesco replied. He gestured outward like a drag queen, almost spilling some of his cocktail.

"Yes, but I spent too much. I lost my mind yesterday."

"You know, Dinky, I'm relieved to hear you admit that."

Francesco wandered over to Stanley and kissed him.

"That's love in action," Graham said.

"Is it your anniversary?" Tony asked. "Is that why we're here?"

"No, it's not our anniversary," Francesco replied. "It's just a good night for celebrating." He kept his gaze with Stanley for a moment longer. There was an unusual calm in his partner's face, even though he'd just come home from work. Francesco then inspected his glass. "We need more martinis."

"I have to drive tonight," said Tony. "No more for me."

"Nonsense," Francesco said. "It's a celebration!"

"But if it's not your anniversary, what are we celebrating?"

"Life!" Francesco sat himself on Tony's armrest. "Help us celebrate, please."

"Go on," Graham teased. "We can taxi home."

"Sweetheart, it's a school night. I have teeth to drill tomorrow."

"But your first patient isn't booked until eleven o'clock. You told me yourself on the way over."

Francesco snatched Tony's glass from his hand. "There you go. No mouths to inspect until after brunch. Martini coming up!"

★

Tony was mellower an hour later. There was still no sign of dinner, but both he and Graham had snacked on cashews which Stanley found in the pantry after the couple enquired about food.

"There's something charming about you both," Francesco said to their guests. "You fit together like a hand in a glove."

Graham burst out laughing. Tony swigged the rest of his martini to stop himself snickering. He raised his empty glass, waiting for another cocktail.

"You have a way with words, Franky." Stanley giggled as he spoke. "*They fit like a hand in a glove!* I know you can do better than that."

"We fit like two birds in a cage," Tony replied.

"No, sweetheart," said Graham. "Birds in a cage are trapped. Neither of us feel trapped."

"Like birds and bees," Stanley suggested.

"Birds don't mate with bees." Graham shook his head.

"And I thought *I* was the overthinker." Stanley looked to Francesco for a response.

"I know what they're like," Francesco said. He lifted his martini from the wooden surface of the bar, forgetting that Tony was still waiting for one to be made. "They're like no other. They're Tony and Graham."

Francesco drank first. Stanley shrugged when he realised Tony was without a glass and then followed his partner's lead. Graham shared his drink with Tony.

"What's the secret to your success?" Francesco asked.

"Our success?" Graham needed clarification.

"Your relationship. What has it been now? Ten years?"

"Sixteen," Tony replied as he stood up and made his way to the bar. He mixed his own drink.

"Sixteen!"

"You know it's been sixteen years, Frank," said Graham. "I've told you many times at the theatre. Don't you listen?"

"How do you keep it fresh? Do you wander?"

Tony cringed, but no one saw.

"As you said, we're a hand in a glove," Graham replied.

"You must have met young?" Stanley asked.

"In our twenties."

"That *is* young," Francesco noted.

"Frank, we've had this conversation." Graham was frustrated.

"Don't mind my old man," said Stanley. "He's forgetful when he's drunk. Now, was it love at first sight?"

"Ah, the charming cliché," Francesco added.

Tony stirred his own cocktail. Francesco noticed and subtly averted his eyes in guilt.

"Love at first sight?" Graham mused. His partner joined him back on the couch. "It's not the sight of someone that you fall in love with, it's their personality. Something clicked within us both."

"We didn't realise it at the time though," Tony said.

"It's as clear as crystal looking back on that day. We couldn't take our eyes off each other, but Tony's looks didn't reel me in. It was the way he carried himself. No, I'm wrong. It wasn't that. It's that we both clicked, and we knew it on some subconscious level. Does that make sense?"

Tony gazed at his lover. "Like you met an old friend. Yet it's your first meeting. A meeting of minds if you like."

"Yeah, that's it."

Francesco and Stanley smiled at each other, but both were privately pondering if this was how it happened for them. Tony stood, stumbling a little as he got to his feet.

"Are you okay?" Stanley asked.

"I need to pee." He sauntered off.

"A couple like you must get hit on all the time," Francesco said.

"Not so much now, but when we were younger, yes," Graham replied. "When we partied harder."

"Did you ever take up an offer?" Stanley asked.

"Hmm. That's a story for another time."

"There're flowers in your bedroom!" Tony yelled from the hallway.

Graham got up to see for himself. His gasp turned into a grin. Stanley joined the couple and encouraged them to move toward the bed and take a closer look.

On both side tables, three tall yellow daisies stood prominently in clear glass vases. The chest of drawers under the window proudly displayed a mixed arrangement of red beauties. Roses were its main feature. Various other flowers, that Graham didn't recognise, held his attention as he felt their petals.

Francesco entered with the drink Tony left behind. Stanley strolled to his partner and casually undid the buttons on his shirt.

"I think it's bedtime," Francesco declared. "Try out the bed, boys. It's very firm."

"Frank, you've got it wrong," said Graham. "I love you as a workmate, that's all. As far as I was concerned, we were just coming for dinner."

"Dinner?" Stanley laughed. "Franky can't boil an egg."

"No!" Tony kept his voice calm. "You didn't think we'd...?"

"Well, you're a beautiful gay couple," Francesco said. "Let me repeat—a beautiful *gay* couple. Are we not your type?"

"Frank, let me speak for both of us," said Graham. "We don't play around. I'm not judging you and Stanley. Each to their own. But I really thought we were coming for dinner until I realised Stan wasn't home to cook. I know you can't cook, Frank, so I started wondering if we were eating out—"

"Hell to dinner." Francesco undid his shirt buttons. "Have some dessert!"

"Can we get out of here?" Tony stressed. "Please!"

"We're sorry, guys," said Stanley. "Frank thought..." He looked to his feet. "I'm not sure what Frank thought. I expected an older couple tonight."

"They are an older couple," Francesco said.

"Yes, Graham and Tony are older than our usual playthings, but I was expecting a couple our own age. Maybe even a few years older."

"Yuck." Francesco looked as if he bit a lemon.

"Franky, we aren't young anymore," Stanley stressed.

"Just young at heart," said Graham.

"Can we leave now?" Tony asked.

"Yeah, I think we should."

Tony dragged Graham out of the bedroom, clutching his arm tight. "Thank you for an entertaining evening. And all the martinis."

"We'll see ourselves out," Graham called before Tony slammed the door.

Stanley eased himself onto the edge of their bed and sat.

"They don't know what they're missing," Francesco said proudly. He made his way back to the bar to make another martini.

His partner didn't follow. He lay back, numb, and mulled through the last five minutes over and over, until sleep saved him from anger.

Chapter Five

Passion

There was a female violinist next to Asher at their dining table this time in Stanley's dream. And although Stanley didn't usually go for classical soloists, he found something hauntingly familiar in the musician's tune.

They were alone this time in the restaurant circled by the crimson curtain, and formal wear was not the attire for tonight. Both wore loose white shirts. Comfortable and classy.

"I know this now," said Stanley, referring to the music. He laughed to himself. "My mother tried to teach me this once, on her piano."

"I didn't know you could play," said Asher.

"I can't. She tried to teach me several times when I was hardly old enough to blow my nose. She wanted a child prodigy."

"Was she selfish?"

"I'm joking. I've told you my mum was special. It was her way of getting me to become captivated with life. Not that I needed help. She inspired me to ask a million questions, and she answered every one."

"Are you still close?"

"Asher, you ask all the questions, yet I know nothing about you."

Stanley glanced at the reservation card on their table. It still displayed THE MIDNIGHT MAN in bold letters. He picked it up to take a closer look and as he did, he noticed a small scar on his hand. *This is, after all, a dream,* he thought, *so this scar must be meaningless.* As he gazed again at his date, the violinist moved away from their table while still playing that familiar tune.

"Why are you called the Midnight Man?"

"Because it's after midnight, Stan."

"You've avoided this question before. What exactly is your purpose in my dreams?"

All of Asher's teeth were on display in the smile he'd summoned. Stanley was taken by his date's mischievous grin, making him feel a little more youthful than his upcoming half-century milestone.

"My jeans don't feel as tight," Stanley said.

"We haven't eaten yet."

"I'm not even hungry." He swirled the red wine in his glass. "Asher, I'm younger, aren't I?"

"It's my present to you. You're in your mid-forties."

"Of course, that's when I grazed myself, right here on my hand. And my jeans are looser. They aren't strangling my gut."

"But isn't your waist size the same now as when you were forty-five? And why were you crucifying yourself four and a half years ago?"

"To answer your first question, Asher, I have a little overhang above my waist. It's the balcony above the toy shop. Too many of my mother's Tuesday dinners. And I wasn't playing martyr when I got that scar. We were doing renovations, trying to go rustic with second-hand timber. And when I picked up a plank of wood, a huge splinter went under my skin. I clenched my teeth in agony as Franky got the tweezers and fished it out. The scar was there for a year or two after that."

"Let me see."

Stanley suspended his hand above the table as Asher studied the wound.

"It's funny how a small thing like a scar can bring back memories," said Asher.

"You're too young to be this wise."

"But you agree with what I said?"

"Perhaps..."

Asher kissed the wound. Stanley wasn't sure whether he should pull his hand back. Asher used his chin to gently trace a path from Stanley's scar to the tip of his thumb. His youthful stubble tickled his admirer.

"Now you're playing with me, my Midnight Man."

"Perhaps..."

"You want to sleep with me."

"I never said that, Stanley."

"But you're thinking it."

Asher gradually let go of Stanley's hand, but Stanley kept it in place for a moment longer. Asher beamed. Stan held his wine in front of him. Asher raised his. Stanley kept an eye on his dinner companion as he sipped, pondering what storyline would guide this dream.

"Would I sound alarmist if I questioned why you didn't go to hospital?" Asher asked. "With a scar that bad, why didn't you get medical attention?"

"Franky and I were drunk. We started sober, but he believed manual labour is best when administered with martinis." Stanley smirked like a thief who'd stolen the queen's treasures.

"You've had such a rich life. I'm envious."

"Yes, perhaps I *once* had a rich life. Hmm." Stanley lowered his head so he could gaze into Asher's eyes. "Now, young man. Who are you, besides a figment of my imagination?"

"I'm someone trying to find what life has in store. That's why we're having these dates. I need to know where I should go next. What my life is all about."

"Continue."

"I have a passion for music." He looked at the violinist. "I've got an invitation to study the flute with an orchestra, but there's no guarantee of working with them after my studies. I don't want to waste years of my life when I could have a decent career."

"You're enchanting, Asher. You're my Pied Piper."

"You're making fun of me."

"No, I'm not. Incidentally, my mother finally got me to play the flute. She paid for the lessons." Stanley felt sad for a moment but didn't understand why. "Passion in all its forms should be what life is about. Hmm. I can't believe I just said that."

"Why? It's great advice."

"Asher, follow your dreams for in them is hidden the gate to eternity."

"That's even better advice."

"My mother used to say that to me a very long time ago. It was her stock phrase." He focused once more on Asher's bewitching smile. "Ironic that *you* are in my dreams. Are you *my* gate to eternity?"

Asher adjusted his posture, sitting perfectly straight like a schoolboy from a forgotten era. "I think passion is your gate to eternity." He picked up the wine bottle and filled their glasses. He then gestured to an opening in the crimson curtain. "I think passion played a big part in your life when you were forty-five."

"You intrigue me, Asher. Sometimes I see you as a boy starting his journey and then you become someone else."

"I'm your dream character, Stan. You can compose me any way you like, but for now I want to see how *you* display passion." He stood with his glass in hand. "Come on. Bring your wine with you. We have a show to catch."

Stanley did as he was told. Through the shadows on the other side of the curtain they heard two distinct voices toasting one another, followed by the sound of clinking glasses. Asher held his glass high. Stanley understood his meaning and toasted their friendship before stepping toward the dialogue in the darkness.

"That's me, isn't it?" Stanley asked. "And that other voice is Franky."

Light appeared on the previously unlit faces, and there were Stanley and Francesco with martinis in hand and paint cans at their feet.

As they watched, Stanley placed his arm around Asher's waist.

★

"I think this is one of my better mixes," said Francesco, holding his martini up to the light to study it.

"Is this healthy?" Stanley asked. "Painting and drinking at the same time? These fumes are deadly."

"Dinky, my love, passion in all its forms is what life is about. Here we are getting creative by painting our new home with this...what is this again?"

"Horizon Blue."

"Like I said, creative with this Horizon Blue colour and warming ourselves with gin and vermouth."

Stanley beamed as Francesco moved behind him and wrapped his free arm around his waist.

★

"Now, that's a smile," Asher noted. "And it's not just your face that's come to life. You're at ease in Franky's embrace."

"We couldn't keep our hands off each other, even when we were renovating."

"What's the matter, Stan? Is this the day you got that scar?"

"Possibly, but that was the furthest thing from my mind just now."

"Then what is it?"

In front of them the loving couple were still in their embrace. Francesco held his martini to Stanley's lips. He sipped, closing his eyes to sense more of this moment.

But then, as if a theatre spotlight had been turned off, the scene turned dark. The scent of frangipani filled the air. Candlelight now lit a new scene in front of them. The floral odour came from incense which burned in the shower while Francesco and Stanley sipped champagne in their bathtub.

"Now we're in for a show!" Asher's grin was more than gleeful.

★

"I can't begin to explain how much you inspire me, Dinky."

"That's because you don't know me as well as you think you do."

"For once, please don't put yourself down. You do things that take me out of my comfort zone."

"I what?"

"You heard me."

"How?"

Francesco carefully chose his words. "You make me the better part of myself, and please let me finish before you interrupt. We walked past that homeless guy the other day and I was ready to keep on going. And we did. We walked on for a block or two until that burger joint. You stopped and I was thinking, *Hell, Stan. We just had dinner.*

"You went inside, and I reluctantly followed, still swearing under my breath at you slowing our journey home. You bought an extravagant meal and stepped out again. I followed you like a faithful mutt while getting frustrated."

"I know what I did, Franky."

"Let me finish. You retraced our steps and gave the meal to the homeless guy."

"And your point is?"

"I wasn't only proud of you, I felt proud within myself. And even though I have no reason to take any credit from what you did, seeing that man reach out and thank you made me realise we all have purpose."

"That's deep for you, Franky."

"I'm not sure you know how much I love you, Dink. You have this effect to me."

Stanley's eyes moistened. He lifted his glass and toasted their love and then looked above him, searching for his own response as if it was floating somewhere near the ceiling.

"Frank, the homeless man was about me facing something."

"And whatever it is, you faced it out of love. But that's not the only reason I admire you, Dinky. You cook for my friends. You selflessly hide in the kitchen until dinner is served and then laugh at the table with everyone else. You light up the room."

"You're exaggerating."

"And you're underselling yourself again."

They both leaned forward and kissed.

"If you see me as someone who lights up your world, then you have to take the credit. Having someone love me is what's giving me strength." Stanley gulped, unintentionally. He then paused to keep his emotions in check. "We've nearly been together for two years and you *make* me, Franky. I haven't felt supported for a very long time and if you knew that deep inside me there's a scared younger man who tries to navigate the world, well..." Stan smirked. "I'm rambling, aren't I?"

"There you go, Dinky. Putting yourself down again." Francesco took Stan's hand and kissed his finger. "That younger man..." He kissed the next finger. "...who's navigating the world..." Then, the next. "...has me by his side." The next. "And together we're a team that will never drift apart."

The candlelight faded.

★

"What are you thinking about?" Asher asked. "Who is that scared younger man you were talking about?"

"That's not what's on my mind."

"Then, what is it?"

"I'm pondering something my mother said." Stanley wanted to walk away from this memory, but something held him there.

"You're seeing your past at a time when you felt passion, but you're thinking of your mum?"

Stanley sighed. "Asher, my mother is right." He stepped away from his Midnight Man.

"About what?"

"Franky is having an affair."

Chapter Six

Party

"I can't believe they came," said Tony to Graham under his breath.

The couple had let Stanley and Francesco through their front door. Graham watched them head to the back of their house where several other friends had congregated.

"Why didn't they un-invite themselves?" Tony continued. "Seriously! They tried to have sex with us. What kind of moronic people hit on you then show up at your party?"

"Darl, Frank still works with me, so it's not strange that they should be here. It's not like I told him not to come."

"But seriously, common decency..."

Francesco zeroed in on a blond guy with a curl dangling over his forehead. This younger man had topped his glass with vodka when Francesco shimmied beside him and leaned against the pantry. Stanley watched his partner without expression. The embarrassment he felt was held within. Despair soon replaced it.

"You're a feisty one," said the blond.

"If you only knew." He walked his fingers on the cedar stone bench top toward the man's glass. "What are you drinking with your vodka?"

"Just soda. I'm Elliot, by the way. And you are...?"

"Francesco, Franky, Frank. Take your pick."

"Franky. It makes you sound young."

"Ouch. I just look old, Elliot. It's the mark of a well lived man."

"Well, Franky, it looks like you've lived a few lifetimes."

"Touché," said Stanley. He went in search of others.

★

"Who is that man chatting up my man?" a guy asked his female friend in the living room.

"That's my man chatting up your man," Stanley replied. "Do you need to rescue Elliot?"

"Trust me," replied the woman. "No one needs to rescue Elliot." She offered her hand. "I'm Lucy, and this is my favourite man in the whole world, Nathan."

"That sounds like quite an honour. I'm Stan, or Stanley if you prefer."

"Do you need a drink, Stan?" Nathan asked.

"I'll get one soon. The truth is, I don't feel like drinking tonight."

"A Coke, perhaps."

"Don't fuss. I'll help myself eventually." He studied the pair. Lucy was adorned in a leopard print dress while her friend wore an ordinary leather jacket, even though it wasn't that cold. They sipped cocktails of some type which Stanley didn't recognise. Nathan leaned into Lucy, wrapping his arm around her as if they were a couple. It wasn't until they eyed him up and down that he asked, "How do you know Graham and Tony?"

"Through Elliot," Nathan said. "My boyfriend knows everyone, and those he doesn't know, he's out to meet. They've been friends for, well, forever. And you?"

"Franky works with Graham at the theatre. They're gossiping girlfriends."

They all watched Elliot who now rested his hand on Francesco's shoulder, standing over him like a high-ranking officer.

"A bit of dominance," Stanley noted. "Franky will like that."

"I should rescue my boyfriend." Nathan turned to Stanley. "Sorry, I didn't mean to make it sound—"

"My man can be an old bore. But be careful. He'll suggest a ménage once you show up."

Nathan smirked as he left.

"You need a drink," Lucy said.

"Honestly, I'm fine."

"Listen. I've been around gay men most of my adult life, and I know when one of my gals needs a drink."

She crouched near the sofa to grab her fluorescent pink handbag. She pulled out a bottle of gin and then tucked her bag under the coffee table. "Easier access," she said.

Elliot entered with a glass of soda water and ice for Stanley. "Nate told me you need a drink."

"Perfect timing," Lucy noted.

"But now Nathan is enduring my bore of a husband by himself," said Stanley.

"We're taking shifts," Elliot replied.

Lucy poured gin into the glass Elliot was still holding for Stanley. Then she topped up her own drink.

"By the way, I'm Stan."

Elliot handed him his drink. "I know. Nate filled me in. Now, we need to do something about this music."

"You shouldn't touch their stereo," Lucy replied. "It's rude."

"Has that ever stopped me?" He strode to the hi-fi. Soon soaring female vocals and a heavy bass beat took over as more Gen Y guests arrived.

★

Stanley stood against the pantry. With gin in hand, he peered into the living room at Nathan and Elliot. Nathan leaned casually against the furthest corner. Elliot pressed into him, their foreheads touching as if all was being said through telepathy.

Nathan closed his eyes and puckered his lips. Elliot answered his call. Their kiss lingered as if they were alone.

Stanley smiled, yet he didn't feel joy. He reached for his mouth and felt its shape as if he were a blind man sensing someone else's features. *Are my lips thin? Is this the smile of a man turning fifty?*

"We only talk to people with the same views, until we reach out of our comfort zone to converse with those who confront us with an opposing view. You know, the opposite of us." Stanley didn't look to see who was talking. He didn't care who else was in the kitchen. "Think of it as a rubber band stretching back and forth. It's how we used to communicate."

Communication, Stanley thought. *If only communication didn't hurt so much.*

Elliot still had his forehead pressed against Nathan's, but they were talking now. It didn't matter what was being said. Stanley knew Nathan's comforting grin showed Elliot that he could converse with him for the next fifty years and Nathan's enthusiasm would never wane.

Stanley recalled Francesco and his words of love in their bathtub, all those years ago. He pictured Franky kissing his fingers and remembered how they attempted to make love in their poky tub.

He traced his finger over his mouth again. This was a content smile. This was Nathan's smile. This was how Stanley used to smile.

His heart sank. It didn't want to stay inside his wretched body. It craved love and laughter. It wanted to fly and find nirvana.

Asher's face came to his mind. *My Midnight Man makes me smile. He's not bitter and cold.* Stanley's hand left his face. He didn't need to feel his mouth. He knew this grin was here to stay.

He brought his drink to his lips and threw the demon liquid down his throat. He quickly poured another as he watched Nathan and Elliot. Little did he know from the hallway, Francesco had been watching his lonely routine.

★

"What's the secret of your seven-year relationship?" Nathan asked Stanley.

"Lack of imagination," he slurred.

Stanley was still propped against the kitchen pantry as it kept him from sliding to the floor. Elliot was by Nathan's side, both more sober than Stan's melancholy self.

"There has to be something more that keeps you and Franky together." Nathan glanced at Elliot. Elliot shrugged.

"Lies." Stanley stared into the distance. "A workable relationship is full of half-truths and dreams you give up on."

"Are you constipated or is that just your personality?" Elliot smirked.

Stanley wandered toward the living room. A few people were dancing, including Graham who was thankful for Elliot's earlier MP3 intervention. Tony was sharing recipes with his workmates, all the while making sure he kept his distance from Francesco who was still talking to Lucy. Both had been joined by a man whose arm-length tattoos had them both fantasising excessively. Stanley then returned to the kitchen pantry and leaned against the wall for support.

"I want to know something," he finally said, waving his finger in the air.

Nathan and Elliot leaned in, in case they had to grab him before he crashed to the ground. Stanley thought they were just listening intently.

"What do you want to know?" Elliot asked.

"What?"

"You said you wanted to know something," Nathan replied.

"Oh yes. Do you guys dabble?"

The couple looked down their noses at one another.

"Do we, Nate?"

"Our bliss is its own reward."

"Get me a bucket," Stanley groaned. "Where's your sense of gay abandon? Seriously! You're hetero-normal piss-weak ants."

"But it works," Nathan replied. His lips met Elliot's briefly.

"Hey, your boyfriend just spent the last hour trying to invite me and Nate into your boudoir, without success." Elliot discreetly gestured toward Francesco. "Do you ever wonder where Franky is when you're not home?"

"Oh, shut up!" Stanley covered his mouth as soon as these words flew out. "Sorry." He removed his hand. "But you can't say you both wouldn't want to trace your fingers up that man's tattoos and see where they lead. And you can. Together. Or go find another couple. Tony and Graham, perhaps. You're young. Go fuck!"

Elliot caressed Nathan's cheek. "Why go out for mince when you have steak at home?"

"Sweetheart, your monogamy-rich sayings have been around since Adam discovered Steve, but none of us gays adhere to them. Half the heterosexuals don't either. So, stop with your kissy antics and grow up a little!"

"I think our happiness is a sore point," said Nathan.

"You think you're happy, you foetus? You'll look back on these days with maturity, eventually, and know full well your happiness was a sham."

Stanley gasped as Elliot stared into his eyes and declared, "Ever heard the saying, 'Grow up, not old'?"

"Yes, and these are the ramblings of an old man," Francesco said.

He and Lucy had entered the kitchen to calm things down. Tony and Graham followed.

"Is everything okay?" Graham asked.

"You could have slept with us," Stanley continued. "You and your Asian boyfriend."

"I have a name," said Tony.

"They obviously didn't sleep with you because they have taste," Elliot replied. "Sorry, Franky. Just trying to…"

Francesco nodded back, smiling to himself. "I think it's time for me and Stan to go home."

He reached to take his inebriated partner by the arm. Stanley pushed him away. Both Lucy and Tony grabbed the drunk guest as he steadied himself. He looked at them and forced a grin.

"Generation Y! Why indeed?" He now waved his hand in the air as if he was on a pulpit. "A generation lost to lack of life experience. Oh, the sky is falling, but how many likes do I have on my post? Aliens have made contact; time for a selfie with my bestie! World War III has started. Oh, but my favourite YouTube star has just uploaded—"

"That's enough, Dinky." Francesco's voice was low yet authoritative. But Stanley wasn't in the mood to feel pushed around.

"You're not here forever, kids! Stop giving in to this disease called monogamy! Go have a life. A real life that doesn't include swiping a screen."

"Shall I call a taxi?" Tony asked.

"A taxi?" Stanley moved forward to stand on his feet, but quickly stumbled so he grabbed the kitchen bench. "A taxi, you say? But why would we want a taxi? I have so many new friends."

"Dinky!"

"Franky, darling. Look! A cutesy couple who need some real men to show them how to do it. We need to pound them tender."

Elliot was about to speak but Nathan calmly placed his finger to his boyfriend's lips.

"I'm sure they don't need mentors," Lucy said.

"They look like they could write the manual," Francesco added, smiling kindly.

"And what's with this leopard print?" Stanley waved his finger up and down Lucy's dress. "The sixties are as stale as broadcast television. Is that your attempt at retro chic?"

Tony grabbed him and quickly escorted him to the front door. Several other males helped.

"Wisdom is lost on the youth!" Stanley shouted from the entrance.

"I am so sorry, Graham," Francesco whimpered, looking as if he'd been told a relative had died.

"No need to apologise for me!" Stanley yelled from outside.

"Sort him out," Graham replied, placing his hand on Frank's shoulder.

"Yes," said Elliot, grinning like a maniac. "True love and retro chic can be confronting to ageing stagnant lives."

Chapter Seven

Shame

Stanley sobbed like a baby.

"What's the matter?" It was Asher's voice.

He opened his eyes. They were sitting on the ground in darkness.

"I'm losing myself, Ash. More than before, I'm losing myself."

Asher handed him a handkerchief, so he mopped the tears from his cheeks as if wiping away the evidence of his shame.

"Steady on, Stan. You'll bruise your face."

He howled louder. Asher crouched and tried to put his arm around him. Stanley pushed him away.

"I'm not worthy of your love. Or anyone's love."

"That's not what I saw the last time we met."

Stanley sat in silence. He didn't know what to say. He sensed a hundred half-baked thoughts whirling inside the tornado in his head. None of them presented a coherent reason for his actions.

Asher sat and waited patiently for Stan's pain to subside. And as the moments lingered, Asher hummed a tune. Stanley recognised the familiar melody. It was the song his mother tried to teach him to play on the piano. The memory soothed him.

"Are you my guardian angel?" Stanley asked.

"Nothing of the sort." Asher placed his hand on Stanley's knee. "If I were your guardian angel, I'd know why you were crying."

Stanley laughed. "That makes sense."

"So, why were you crying?"

"I made a fool of myself at a party. Some twisted bitter version of myself spewed venom in every direction."

"Why?"

He pondered. "You saw the happier version of me and Franky the last time we met. That's not us today. Today, we're ugly old queers, with me being the eldest—"

"But not the ugliest."

Stanley grinned. "I don't think I'm the right cut for a relationship."

"From what I saw, you *had* something with Franky, once upon a time."

"I'm not sure we can have it again."

"Do you want to?"

"I'm not sure about that either."

Asher gave Stanley a pensive glance.

"Then maybe that's why I'm your Midnight Man. Perhaps this is where your perfect world exists."

There was that title again. Midnight Man. Stanley didn't feel like battling for an answer to what it meant.

"You said last time you believe your mother is right," said Asher. "About Franky having an affair."

"I know his tastes. It will be a younger man who makes him feel he's in control. A himbo, for sure."

Asher stood, reaching for Stanley's hand at the same time. "So, while he's chasing his youth, you have me."

"Do you want to sleep with me, Ash?"

"I didn't say that."

"But it sounds like it's what you're thinking." He took Asher's hand and stood. "No, seriously, Ash. Is that why you're here? To romance me?"

"Hey, it's your dream. You tell me."

"I don't want this dream to end. Otherwise, I'll wake in my *real* nightmare."

"When did the man who kissed your fingers in the bathtub become your nightmare?"

Stanley gulped. He wasn't sure he wanted to answer. Asher waited for his reply.

"About two years ago. We organised a date night. Dinner at an upmarket burger joint followed by a bad superhero movie. I showered, changed, popped on a new shirt and some aftershave. Then I waited. He didn't call or text. I turned the news on. I watched a ridiculous reality show. I checked my phone. Eventually I went to bed. He never mentioned what happened and I never asked."

Asher caressed Stanley's cheek with the tip of his thumb. He moved his lips close to Stan's, but Stan forced a grin and looked away.

"My timing's off." Asher took Stanley's chin and gently moved his head so he could study his eyes.

"It's okay," Stanley replied. "There's a lot to process."

The scene changed. Asher drove as Stanley gazed into the night. There was something comforting about being a passenger. He was with someone he hardly knew yet trusted wholeheartedly.

"Asher, is this what a nervous breakdown feels like?"

"I don't know. I've never had one."

Stanley sunk into the bucket seats, a moment of comfort from his troubled thoughts. He felt the smooth armrests on his door, moving his hand back and forth as if he was stroking a lover.

He listened. That tune Asher hummed earlier came to life with an orchestra performing through a state-of-the-art speaker system.

Swank terrace houses whisked past on a street with never-ending trees. Not a garbage can nor a stray dog in sight. *This is an impeccable neighbourhood*, Stanley thought.

"Where are we going?" he asked. He was feeling better.

"We're making a good impression on my musician friends."

"Oh. I guess I owe you some kindness in return." Stanley ran his fingers through his hair. It seemed thicker. "Am I younger?"

"You're forty."

"I was single when I was forty." He laughed to himself.

"Well, tonight you're my sugar daddy. I need you by my side."

They arrived at a huge brass gate which opened of its own accord. The automobile's headlights beamed into the distance, gradually displaying the driveway made of chic charcoal bricks. The house eventually came into view, a stylish marriage between white plaster and natural timbers.

Stanley's eyes widened. He didn't know anyone this wealthy. He stepped out of the car, and after he felt the sturdiness of the door, he watched it as it closed. He was in awe of the artistry of Asher's black sports car.

"Come," said the young man. "We're already late."

"Do you have an exclusive arrangement with Asher?" asked a curly haired man with pepper tones.

He was one of three middle-aged guests who Stanley was unsuccessfully trying to converse with at the dinner table. A twinkling chandelier hung low over the food, and due to Stanley's elongated height, he was the only one who had to lower his head to see the eyeline of whomever was talking to him.

"Do we have an exclusive relationship?" Asher repeated the man's question. "We've never talked about it. Do we, Stan?"

"But on your travels...?" said the woman in the red dress. Her face was so stretched she looked mummified.

"Asher, don't you get to play with the twinks or the otters or whatever you call people your own age? And Stanley, don't you immerse yourself in steam in each new city you visit?" She had a wry smile.

"We haven't travelled," Asher replied.

"You haven't travelled?" said a man with his hair slicked back. He was the only one in a dinner jacket and a bowtie. "Why don't you take this young man abroad, Stanley?"

"Um, I'm not sure where to take him."

"I'm amazed at you," said the curly-haired one. "Think back to when you were twenty-one. The romance of a round-the-world ticket in your hand and affairs in every major city. Prague, for instance!"

"Oh, I remember Prague." The woman's voice was husky as she spoke. "Cobblestone streets. The Charles Bridge. And Robert."

"Robert?" asked the guest in the dinner jacket. His tone nostalgic.

"Oh, he had fingers that could reach as far as the moon. He played me like a double bass. Plucked me when I needed it, then forced his bow across me when I demanded it."

"You devilish woman."

"I need adventure," Asher confessed. He gazed at Stanley wistfully.

"Go to Barcelona!" the curly-haired one demanded. "It's full of life and full of art. It's the perfect place for a dreamer like you."

"And who did you dream with in Barcelona?" the woman enquired.

"Felipe. Oh, Felipe. He was my first."

"First what?" Stanley asked before he realised the answer for himself. The woman giggled.

"He purred like a race car ready to burn down the track—"

"And then he burned up your track," Stanley joked.

The woman groaned.

"Crude, but true," the curly-haired man replied.

"Take me somewhere, Stan," Asher pleaded.

"Yes, Stanley," the man, who was now caressing his bowtie, said. "Show him *your* New York."

"My New York? I'm not from New York."

"But you have memories of New York?"

"I've never been to New York."

"Nonsense. Everyone's been to New York. I suspected you weren't well travelled, but surely New York?"

"Where have you been?" the woman asked.

"I've been to Auckland."

"You've been to New Zealand!" The curly-haired man snickered with each word. "You're so *cultured*."

"Tell me, Stanley," the woman continued. "Was there excitement and adventure in Auckland?"

"It's very cosmopolitan," he replied. He tried his best to sound educated.

"And which tall, handsome sheep farmer did you meet?"

He studied Asher's face before he answered. The young man looked as if he'd once believed in Superman, but now knew only Clark Kent was real.

"I didn't get time for romance. I was a teenager. My mother took me there for a family wedding."

"Oh my," the woman said. She stood and made her way to the bar, seizing a bottle of gin. "What life experience can you show our Asher? He's in his prime. There's a world out there dying to make love with him. Where do you exist in that world, Stanley?"

"I love him."

"Love is a four-letter word." She returned and poured the gin in everyone's wineglass, liberally. "It's here today and..." She snapped her fingers. "...gone the next. Here's my advice to you, Asher." She crouched next to him. "Always find people in life who advance you in mind, body, and soul. And baby, discard anyone who's not up to the challenge."

★

"How did we get here?" Stanley asked Asher.

"It's a dream. We've jumped time and place."

They lay next to each other, naked, on a plush heart-shaped bed.

"My imagination is so clichéd." Stan rolled onto his side, gazing at the young man while feeling like a loser. "My imagination and my life are just one big cliché."

Stanley quivered as Asher stroked his cheek. "Why haven't you travelled?"

"It wasn't important to me."

"Then, where do you find your passion?"

"If I don't find it through you, then I think I'll be forever lost." Stanley stared into the distance.

"Is that why you told that woman you loved me?"

"Ash, a moment ago I was facing up to how alone I'd become after regretting what I'd done at a party, and now your snooty friends have judged me."

"And how do you feel?"

"Like I've got nothing to prove to the characters in my dream life—"

"Hmm."

"Except for you, of course. Yet I still have everything to prove in my waking life."

"Is it a challenge you can face, Stan?"

"I have to apologise to Graham and Tony. Perhaps even Francesco if he'll bother to notice. I'm not sure. I don't think I care anymore."

He contemplated the younger male form next to him. Even with his forty-year-old body, Stanley couldn't work out why a twenty-one-year-old would be remotely interested. Paler skin. A grey hair here and there. Nose hairs that extended like Triffids. Loose flesh around his belly-button.

But then he sensed Asher loved the attention and at that moment, Stanley felt more alive than he did in his waking life.

"Asher, why do you want me?"

"What makes you think I want you?"

"An educated hunch."

Asher shared a loving smile. "Experience. That's why any guy my age beds an older man. Sexual experience."

"Your friends think I have no passion."

"There are different types of passion." He kissed Stanley's cheek. "Like the passion of a lonely man…" He kissed his neck. "A lonely man who's in a long-term relationship…" He kissed his nipple. "A relationship where passion has stopped." He kissed his navel. "So, this lonely man needs to hear himself breathe."

Asher opened his mouth wide. Stanley exhaled.

Chapter Eight

Promiscuity

Roast turkey was the dish of the night when Stanley took his chair at his mother's dining table.

"Carve for me, will you, dear?" Adelaide asked. She held an imposing chef's knife.

He stood, took the knife, and sank the blade into the bird. Juices flowed, oozing like treacle.

"You seem happier than usual," she said.

"I'm happy every time I see you, Mother."

"No. There's something different tonight."

"You're imagining it."

"A mother knows her son. In fact, I think I know what's going on. How many roast potatoes would you like?"

She took the tongs and placed several on his plate before he could answer.

"What do you think is going on, Mother?"

"I've known you all your life, so don't think you can keep anything from me." She scooped peas onto his plate. "Gravy?"

"I can serve myself, oh woman of great knowledge."

"You may laugh at me, but I see through you like an X-ray."

Stanley sat, pulling his chair meticulously into the table. He grinned at his mum before poking his fork into the poultry and placing it into his mouth. He chewed.

Adelaide's lips tightened as she watched her son eat. Eventually she got up, opened her newest bottle of sherry, and brought it back to the table. She poured and then sat with her glass hovering above her untouched dinner.

"Do you want me to ask you something, Mother?"

"Did I say that?"

"It's just a feeling I have. That feeling of 'I've brought something up and my son isn't taking the bait'."

"Amuse yourself, Stanley."

She prodded a drumstick with her fork.

"It won't come to life."

He ate for a minute longer before she tapped her painted canary-yellow fingernails on the table. He kept chewing while he watched her.

"Okay, Mother—"

"Don't talk with your mouth full."

He swallowed.

"Okay, Mother, what is it you want to tell me about myself?"

"You're single."

"I'm what?"

"That joke of a man has left you. So, you're single and happy. Now go find a real man. One who has travelled."

Stanley coughed. Adelaide passed her glass of sherry to him. He gulped a mouthful.

"Franky is still in my life."

"So, he hasn't run off with his lover?"

"Mum, *I'm* his lover." He kept a stern face even with his suspicions.

"And who is *your* other lover?"

Stanley coughed again and then took another sip of sherry before staring at his mother.

"I told you I know my son. If you're not single, then who is your new lover?"

He didn't answer. She was prepared to wait, sipping her drink as if everything was harmonious at her table. The Midnight Man's face appeared in his mind. He snickered quietly to himself.

"His name is Asher."

"I knew it. A mother knows. He has a cultured name. What does he do?"

"He's studying to play with an orchestra."

"What instrument?"

Stanley tapped his knife on his plate, unintentionally. "The flute."

"Hmm. Isn't he too old for a career change? Son, I know that grin. How young is he? Thirty-five?"

"Not much younger."

"Thirty?"

"Lower."

"You cheeky monkey." She nodded, approvingly. "He's twenty-one, isn't he?"

"How did you know?"

She poured sherry into his wineglass. "Like mother, like son."

He dropped his cutlery. A bit of gravy splattered on the tablecloth, but his mum didn't seem to mind.

"When did you date a twenty-one-year-old?" Stanley asked.

"When your father was having his affair. And for the record, the young man propositioned *me*." She tapped her fingernails on the stem of her glass. "Please tell me, Stanley, that *he* propositioned *you*."

"He did."

"So, our circumstances are the same. Your father was being unfaithful, and Francesco is being unfaithful. And a twenty-one-year-old will make you believe in yourself until the next one comes along."

"Mother, you weren't facing fifty when Dad was cheating."

"Son, I come from an age when midlife crisis was a sport. Men ran off with their secretaries. Older women played Mrs Robinson. I'm not judging you, Stanley, because I know twenty-one is not your thing. But an affair is better than taking your relationship with Francesco seriously."

He carved a potato and placed the piece in his mouth. He chewed with purpose.

"You're speechless, Stanley."

"I'm trying to put this all into perspective, Mother."

"What is Asher like?"

"It's hard to say. He's twenty-one. Sometimes he's young and other times he's full of wisdom. His personality is hard to pin down."

"It's still developing. But to him he's a little wiser than he was at eighteen, and more idealistic than he'll be at twenty-five." A small tear appeared, threatening to smear Adelaide's makeup. "Romance is the forgotten casualty in life. Work, money, assets—they're the demons that take away people's souls."

"They're necessary demons to those who don't have them."

"But you're turning fifty, my son. And you're looking back to finalise all the elements that make up your life." She gestured vaguely to the space they inhabited. "You have property, albeit with a cheating whore—"

"Mother!"

"My twenty-one-year-old was a breath of fresh air who entered my life when I needed him most. He worked hard at sophistication while I encouraged him to just be himself."

"You encouraged him *not* to be sophisticated?"

"I *do* have a heart, Stanley, no matter what you believe. As I was saying, he came to me when I needed him most. And it sounds like Asher is here to help you rethink your life. Don't ignore the message the universe is trying to tell you."

Stanley was about to speak when his mother's last words sunk in. "He's definitely from *some* universe." He chuckled. "Mother, what life lesson did your twenty-one-year-old teach you?"

"That if you don't play it right, age can be your nemesis. That thinking all your major achievements are a thing of the past can be your undoing. That what you know and what you've done have value, especially to those who haven't experienced what you have to share."

"That's a lot of lessons."

"No, Stanley. If you really listen to what I just said, it's just one lesson. The hidden meaning behind the fountain of youth."

The dutiful son nodded gracefully. He only half understood.

"Who was he?"

She pushed her plate away and waved her glass of sherry in the air. "He was my saviour. The man who made me see there was a new beginning."

"Yes, Mum, but who was he?"

"Hewett. One of my friends' sons. Oh, don't look at me like that, Stanley. It shows you've led a sheltered life." She gazed at her sherry as if her recollections were presenting themselves inside the glass. "We kept it secret. I'm not one to be the subject of gossip. You see, he showed me my worth as an elder, and in the bedroom, he was a willing student."

"Mother!"

"A good man is hard to find, Stanley. Even if he's just an affair, he'll sparkle in your memory like a wedding ring."

"How did he seduce you?"

Her grin was infectious. "I was visiting his mother and he happened to come in from *somewhere*, so after a bit of chitchat, I gave him a lift back to his place. In the car one thing led to another and let's just say..." She watched her finger tracing a pattern on the tablecloth. "He was there as my confidant after I found out about your father's affair. He listened, getting a grasp on the mess we make of our marriages. He learned from my mistakes. At least, I think he did."

Stanley pushed back his chair yet didn't leave the table.

"There's power in age, my son. It's not a death sentence. It's a blessing."

Chapter Nine

Forgiveness

Stanley found the pub that Francesco had mentioned and stayed outside. He felt as vulnerable as a bullied schoolboy. *I'm going to do this,* he thought. *If not for me, for Asher.* He instantly knew how ludicrous it was to think about his midnight lover at this moment. It was not as if Asher was watching Stanley from the dream realm. But the concept consoled him.

Tony and Graham would be inside the bar, both enjoying a glass of wine and a hearty meal. At least that's what Stanley was told by Francesco. Whenever Graham wasn't rostered to work on Wednesday night, he and his partner relaxed here at their favourite queer venue.

Stanley searched for courage. After five minutes, Stanley entered the pub and made his way toward the dining area. Butterflies were crashing into each other inside his stomach, for Tony and Graham were not alone.

Lucy was the first to notice Stan, and at that moment he knew he couldn't turn back and run. In his mind, Lucy's eyes were piercing him with laser beams, but from

Lucy's point of view, she was simply perplexed at why he was here. She asked Graham if they were expecting company.

"This is going to be an interesting three minutes," Tony replied on Graham's behalf.

"Now, now," Graham said.

"Oh look," said Elliot. "It's the queen who goes beyond drama." His voice was louder than it should have been.

"Come now," said Nathan.

"I didn't expect you *all* to be here," Stanley whimpered.

"Who were you expecting?" Elliot asked. "An army of subservient supporting cast all waiting for your next star turn?"

"He's actually come to apologise," said Graham.

"This should be good. Head held high. Holding back the tears. Academy Award stuff!"

"Elliot!" Nathan grumbled.

"I deserve it. Everything you've said, Elliot, and more." Stanley was surprised how easily these words came. "I'm going through a strange phase at the moment and what I said the other night, well, it had nothing to do with any of you."

Lucy smiled. Elliot crossed his arms. The others leaned forward.

"I've been feeling lost, like my life is off track. I'm on a train heading into a tunnel and the darkness scares me. Yeah, Elliot, I am sounding dramatic."

"Yes, you are," he replied. "But good use of metaphor."

"Are you the train, or the damsel in distress tied to the track?" Lucy asked.

Stanley shivered. "I don't think I'm waiting for the collision, but boy, what you just said feels true. What made you say it?"

"I know my gay boys. I've seen that look of desperation before. And if it makes you feel better, I accept your apology."

"Thanks, Lucy, but you got the least of my tirade." He choked on the last word.

"Are you okay?" Tony asked.

"Sit with us," said Nathan.

"Yes, sit with us," said Elliot. He pulled out a bar stool. "Have you eaten?"

"Why? Am I the condemned man about to have his last meal?"

"You *are* dramatic, but funny. Stan, my bark is worse than my bite."

"It's true," said Nathan. "But when he bites it's more fun."

"You two are a perfect match," Stanley noted. He tried to grin.

"Then sit down and tell us how perfect we are," Elliot replied. "Can I get you a gin and soda?" He didn't wait for an answer. He headed for the bar.

"It looks like you're drinking with us," said Lucy.

Part of Stan wanted to sprint out of the front door as fast as humanly possible, but something cemented his feet to the floor, while something else was gently tugging him toward the empty bar stool. He cautiously made his way to his seat. As he sat, he didn't know who to look at. His uncertain smile caught Tony's attention.

"What made you decide to apologise?" Tony asked.

"Payback."

"Payback?" Tony was irked by his answer.

"No. I mean, the payback happened to me." The others shared puzzled glances. "No, I mean karma. Karma happened to me. Over dinner."

"What dinner?" Graham asked. "Who upset you? Frank never mentioned it."

"Frank wasn't there."

"Oh."

"My mother's. I do dinner with Mum on Tuesdays and there were guests there," Stan lied, but it was easier than explaining snooty dream characters. "Anyway, her demon guests made me feel inadequate because I haven't lived a traveller's life. And so, I'm sorry if I made any of you, or Elliot for that matter, feel inadequate for just being born into a certain generation."

"I never feel inadequate," Elliot announced as he returned with Stan's drink. "And Nate is more than adequate. What are we talking about?"

"Stanley felt inadequate," Nathan replied.

"You're right. I *feel* inadequate. That's why I acted like an arsehole at Graham and Tony's party. Those dinner guests brought the truth home to me. Sorry, guys. I was the arsehole guest."

"Well, you're far from an arsehole now," Tony replied, and for the first time, he gave Stanley a genuine smile.

"Thank you."

"What did those demon dinner guests say to you?" Graham asked.

"Who were these dinner guests?" Elliot asked. "I've missed part of the conversation."

"It doesn't matter who they were. It's the way they made me feel. They'd travelled to all these exotic cities and I've only been to New Zealand."

"New Zealand's majestic," Tony said. Another genuine smile.

"But these people were talking up New York and Barcelona and the affairs they had in those cities. And somehow, I never passed 'Go'. I never collected my two hundred dollars."

"What's he talking about?" Graham asked.

"It's a Monopoly reference," Lucy replied.

"I'm sounding foolish. Sorry I bothered you. I'll drink and leave."

"Stanley, get whatever it is off your chest," said Tony. "Don't leave before you say what needs to be said."

"Okay." He shared a gracious look. "I used to have a *life*. When I was a child, I had passion. A hunger for life. You see, I have, or had, rather, the most magical mother. No, you can stop looking sympathetic. She's still alive, but she's different to the mother I had when I was growing up. She took me to the theatre when other kids went to the movies. She took me to galleries and concerts. All sorts of concerts. That should've been enough for those wretched dinner guests. But what I'm getting at is I feel my life stopped sometime after twenty-one, and I'm not sure why."

"Your life must have picked up again after meeting Franky." Graham's voice became quieter by the end of the sentence.

"He's not perfect. We used to..." Stanley took a large swig of his gin. "Nathan, Elliot, learn from Graham and Tony. Live your life! Travel. Experience your dreams together. Don't let anything end the passion."

There was silence for a while. Both couples held hands and reflected. Lucy's finger circled the top of her wineglass while she thought about a man she'd met, but as yet hadn't told the others. She quietly wished for this to be the one.

"I'm sorry to ruin your night out." Stanley was hardly audible. Only Nathan and Elliot really took note of what he said.

"You've added something unique to our night," Nathan replied.

"Dramatic, but unique," said Elliot. "I'm beginning to like you."

Stanley stood, took one last gulp of his gin, and said, "Sorry for my behaviour at the party. I was a loser and if I've learned anything tonight it's that I'm not. I have a need to live my best life, and I have someone in my life who can help me."

Graham sensed Stan was talking about someone other than Frank but gave him the benefit of the doubt.

"I've never said this," Stanley continued, "but I look up to Tony and Graham. You're the blueprint of a long-term relationship, and Nate and Elliot, you're the building blocks. And Lucy, you're someone's charmer. The great woman who will make some man very lucky. Again, I'm sorry for being an idiot at the party but one day I'll show you my better self."

"You just did," said Tony.

"We forgive you," said Lucy.

Elliot raised his drink. Stanley left shortly after.

It was cold outside, but he didn't feel the chilled air on his cheeks. He was winning, finally, taking his first step in the right direction for more years than he could remember.

He stopped to gaze at a coat in a store window. Navy, long and stylish. It was him—the new him. The debonair version that had been misplaced somewhere.

Mental note. Come back and buy this jacket.

He stepped closer to the display and caught his reflection in the window. He was taken by his own proud smirk. "I'm reborn," he said out loud. No one was around to comment. He continued strolling down the street.

Stanley was struck with a happy memory. He recalled being at the circus with his mother. A fire breather blew flames toward him, and he welcomed the warmth with each flare. An elephant staggered. Its feet thumped the dirt as it circled the stage.

A girl somersaulted through the air and grabbed the trapeze in the nick of time. Her male companion, who was waiting to take her arm as she swung toward the steady platform, had a bulge in his pants that could rival an ant hill. Stanley was transfixed.

The elephant trumpeted as it passed, yet Stanley wasn't fazed. He had found something of himself in that acrobat's mound. A gift he wanted to unwrap, and even though Stanley was only fifteen, he yearned to play with a new toy. A succulent toy.

You'll go blind if you keep thinking those thoughts, his mother said.

He remembered his mother's cheeky approval of his sexuality in that moment. It began an acceptance of himself he was thankful his mother instigated with those words.

"Do you have a few dollars?" The voice was gruff.

Stanley's memories ceased. In contrast to his own fashionable footwear was a man, about the same age as Stan, sitting barefoot on the pavement, dishevelled. It was hard to tell what colour his stained and sullied coat originally was. Strands of greasy hair hid half his face.

Stanley reached into his pocket and froze suddenly. He looked left and right. He was halfway down an alley but didn't know how he got there. His memory of his first penile infatuation had led him through a shortcut to the bus shelter. It didn't feel right.

"Please, sir. I need to eat."

The man stared at Stanley, gritting his teeth. His outward gasp signalled he had given up hope, even with this random potential saviour with sleek footwear standing in front of him. Once again Stanley looked left and right. Light seeped into the alley from either side. He let out a breath. Then another and another, each getting deeper until his voice grunted through each exhale.

"Sir, are you okay?"

Stanley ran, heading back to the street where he'd started reminiscing about circus elephants and male bulges. His legs accidently kicked a kink in the pavement, causing him to stumble. He didn't fall. He kept running. He passed the window with the stylish coat as more audible sounds came from his mouth. None of them held any meaning. He crashed into a passer-by who yelled at him. Stanley didn't glance back. He finally ran out of puff and bent over to catch his breath.

He wanted to cry but searched for calm. *It's only a homeless man.* Fragmented memories flooded his head. None of them connected to explain his fear.

Chapter Ten

Theatre

Stanley peered back into the alley, squinting his eyes so he could focus on the homeless man.

"What are you doing?" It was Asher's voice.

"Trying to face something from the safety of my dream world."

"Is it important?"

"Why? What have you got planned for me?"

"A happy memory."

"How old will I be?"

"Very, very young."

A slim version of Adelaide strolled past the alley, holding the hand of an excited boy.

"That's me!" Stanley followed his mother as Asher rushed to catch up.

"Your mum was really attractive."

"She still is."

As Adelaide and her son turned a corner, Stanley and Asher stopped in their tracks. Across the road, a brick building with glass doors stood between a pub and a diner. His mother and his young self sauntered in. In bold black letters above the entrance were the words *The Women*.

"What's the deal with that shirt you were wearing?" Asher asked.

"It was paisley. A print popular in the seventies."

"It looks like purple and green sperm swimming in opposite directions. And did all women wear hats back then?"

"Mother did. The bigger the better." He chuckled as he turned toward Asher. "She struggled with her hat inside the theatre that day. She placed it in her lap, but it annoyed her, so she placed it at her feet but then worried it would get dirty. In the end I popped it in my lap just to keep her quiet. It didn't bother me. The play took my attention."

"What's it about?"

"Friendship and backstabbing. And the 1930s. I fell in love with deco that day. A boy, the arts, and the mother who opened his world. That was a good day. One of many from my childhood." Stanley straightened his stance. "Asher, we're off to the theatre!"

He took Asher's hand and led him across the road. The old men in the pub shouted angry remarks as they rushed by. Asher stared at them blankly. They entered the glass doors where inside the overuse of the colour orange was apparent.

"Did older men lead younger men into theatre foyers in the seventies?" Asher tried to stand still. "Those men were yelling at you as if you were committing a crime."

"Who cares? In my dream I'll do as I please."

Stanley dragged Asher past the box office to the young girl who collected tickets at the door. Her jacket was designed from an old flag, cut up to give her patchwork elegance.

She gestured to the men to enter. For some reason they didn't require tickets. Inside there just happened to be a seat behind Adelaide and her son. Asher and Stanley sat as Adelaide wrestled with her large white hat.

Many older people were here at the matinee which made Stanley remember that on this day, his mother rang his school saying he was too sick to attend. She often did this when she felt like a cultured day with her son. Several gay men in horizontally striped shirts referred to each other by the women's names used in the play, before they took their seats.

Love immersed Stanley as the show began. This was the calm he needed. The boy in front of him was captivated as Manhattan socialites gossiped about men and mistresses. Young Stanley laughed when his mother laughed, although he didn't understand every joke, and chuckled at odd times when he found amusement. He even tried on his mother's hat but took it off when the rim obscured his view.

As some of the classier women entered the stage, little Stanley whispered to his mother, commenting on the way one had done her hair or another looked in a particular dress. He was attracted to the actress who seemed more butch than the others yet held her poise without critique from the other characters.

Older Stanley noted Asher's fascination with the stage and not in his mother or younger Stan, so he eased back and watched the remainder of the first act.

"You've done well," said the woman in the red dress. She appeared next to Stan.

"You picked a good play," said the man with curly hair next to her.

"Do you have to be in this dream?" Stanley whispered. "This is a happy memory for me."

"We're just here to tell you we approve," the woman said. "At least, in this dream. The next time we meet things will be back to normal."

As little Stan giggled at another line to show how sophisticated he was, the audience and the cast slowly faded, leaving Stanley and Asher alone in the theatre.

"When you leave this dream, I'll come here and see how it ends." Asher was wide-eyed.

"You liked it?"

"I know why you were enchanted. I need to know what happens next."

Stanley ruffled Asher's hair. "I became the parent today. Just like my mother."

"I have no idea what you mean."

"I brought culture into your life, Ash. You were my little Stanley, and I was my mother." He looked at the empty stage. "I'm so glad I relived this. It's given me an idea."

"What are we doing next?"

"Not we. I'm toying with an idea but I'm not sure I want to go through with it."

Asher frowned. "Why would you want to take Francesco on a date?"

"I'm not sure. But I'm facing the fact that this is my dream world, and this shouldn't be where I find the most joy."

★

Stanley woke. Francesco snored gently. Stanley rose quietly, put on his robe, and snuck into their study. He fired up the computer and searched the plays being performed in town.

"I knew it!" he blurted. He listened for more of Francesco's snores. His partner hadn't woken. "I knew it," he said at low volume.

The Women was playing at a small theatre. Stanley fetched his credit card.

He sensed dread as his finger hovered above the keyboard where the number 2 was. He had every intention of buying two tickets and planning dinner and a show with Francesco. He double checked Franky's roster. He wasn't working Tuesday night. And Stanley knew his mother would be relieved she didn't have to venture out to her North Shore apartment and cook a roast for her son.

Should I take Mother instead?

The screen went back to the home page. Stanley had paused too long in his indecision. He started again. This time he bought the tickets yet was still unsure he was doing the right thing. It turned out there was a restaurant promoted on the site which specialised in early sittings so its patrons could eat before showtime. He sent them an email and requested a romantic table for two.

"Why am I doing this?"

He thought of that version of Franky who sat with him in the tub many years ago. Then he saw Asher's wide-eyed youthful face in his mind.

"I have to live in reality. I have to. I really have to."

Chapter Eleven

Henry

Henry looked at his naked self in the full-length mirror. He pinched his flabby stomach. Too much flesh was in his hand. He turned his back to the mirror, looking over his shoulder at his arse. He pinched that too. He could have been kneading dough.

More of me to love!

He opened his wardrobe and pulled out a shirt. His date would arrive shortly. Henry had just finished showering, using the citrus soap he had been given as a gift by the man he was waiting for. As his hands reached the last button of his shirt, he looked to his dick.

Well, friend, another man chasing his dreams. Let's see where this one leads.

He left the mirror and chose his underwear. The front door buzzer sounded. He found a tight pair of white briefs and put them on. He reached for his jeans and only got one leg into them as he pressed the intercom to check if it was Francesco at the door. It was. Henry let him in while struggling with his belt buckle.

"You're taking them off already? My, we are horny!"

Francesco kissed Henry and made his way to the sofa.

"You're early."

"Dinky goes straight to his mum's after work on Tuesdays. Mother and son night. So here I am. More time for lovin'."

"You know, Franky, it kills the romance when you refer to him."

"It kills the romance whenever I'm with him."

"Franky!"

Henry shook his head before heading to the kitchen. He opened the oven door to see how crisp the roast was. The aroma caused Francesco to moan.

"I'm sure it's succulent, just like you, Henry."

"If that's your best compliment, no wonder the passion has died in your relationship. I hope this Dinky chap is also playing around."

"What a weird thing to say."

"No, it's not." Henry returned to the living room. "If I knew your partner was screwing around, the irony would be delicious."

"Believe me, he's too witless to screw around."

"I don't believe that. From the way you talk about him, I think he knows."

"I doubt it."

"And I doubt you're a good judge of character."

"Can we stop? This is supposed to be a date. Not a press conference."

Henry laughed. "You have a dark side, Franky. It's sweet but it scares me sometimes."

Francesco didn't have a comeback. This surprised him. So, he gazed at Henry unfazed by his accusations and searched for the desire he'd felt the first time they shared passion.

Lust hadn't presented itself when Francesco first spoke to Henry. It was conversation that intrigued Francesco as Henry presented the same balanced view on life Stanley had, just without the neurotic slant. Yet it was lust that broke the ice when Henry brought Francesco home.

Henry hadn't felt a yearning for a while, but as Francesco was insistent on making love when they struck a casual conversation at, of all places, a laundromat, Henry thought *Why not?*

When Francesco admitted there was someone in his life, Henry simply rolled his eyes, thinking, *Here we go again. Another one.* He'd gotten used to the fact that men in failed relationships fell for him, or at least, thought they had. Henry was no fool. He knew this would be another passing phase. But it was better than going to bed alone, and he loved nutting out what was going on in the minds of his lovers.

"Thank you for not using his real name," Henry said. "It shows respect."

"If I used Dinky's real name it would make me the bad guy."

"That doesn't make sense. You're using his pet name. His lovey-dovey name. That bears more weight than his real name, surely? Don't you feel guilty?"

"Dinky rolls off the tongue. Using his real name would make what we're doing..."

"Would make what we're doing...seem sordid? Frank, you can't pretend you're not cheating. Guilt is going to seep in somewhere."

"But you're the one who asked me not to use his real name. Don't tell me *you're* not avoiding guilt."

"Hmm. Something I'll have to consider."

The grimy plates had been left on the dining table stacked in a pile with the greasy cutlery on top. The fancy crystal glasses were half full. Henry didn't get the chance to clean up. Francesco's compliments, and the sumptuous red wine, had penetrated the veneer of control on the man who lived alone in his rental. Francesco lay on the bed, content, until he gauged Henry's mood had changed.

"What's the matter?"

"Seven years."

"What's seven years?"

"Franky, you're so disconnected from your own relationship you haven't noticed you've been with him for seven years."

"We just had sex and you're thinking about Dinky?"

"This is about sex, Frank. You're going through the seven-year itch. And if Dinky has any sense, he'll be screwing around too."

Francesco stared at the ceiling. "Well, if it makes you happy, yes, maybe Dinky is screwing around too." He closed his eyes and grinned. "Henry. Lovely Henry. I'm here with you, seven-year itch or not. You excite me. You fulfil me."

"I fulfil you?"

"You do. Yeah, it sounds corny, but you do."

"You're gammin. I'm not stupid, Frank. If I fulfilled you, you would have left your man and freed him from your exploits."

"Sweetheart, this is unlike you."

"No. This is exactly like me."

"Do you have to get all *conversational* on me?"

Henry sat up and propped himself against his pillow. "What does love mean?"

"Huh?"

"In your own words, Frank, what does love mean?"

Francesco knew he was on thin ice. *Is it a full moon?* he thought. *That must be the reason for another of Henry's 'holier than thou' moments.* He looked again to the ceiling. It seemed meditative.

"Okay, Frank, if you can't answer what love is, then tell me, why have you fallen out of love with your man?"

"I can't put my finger on it. People drift apart sometimes. It just happens."

"But you must have done some soul searching. You must know the reasons."

"Dinky's obscure. At first it was charming. Now it's just obscure."

"Obscure, hey?" Henry lifted the bedspread and covered his exposed body.

"You don't know him. Trust me, my man is obscure."

"Have you ever been in love?"

"*You* light my fire."

"You're avoiding the question. Besides, I light your fire because I remind you of something you think you lost."

"Do we have to go down this path? For once, can't we just hold each other after sex?"

"No, Franky. You intrigue me."

"Yeah, I know. But not in the way I'd like."

"Now, answer me. What does love mean to you?"

"There's love in what we do."

Henry rose. "This is a pointless conversation, Frank. You're not being open with me."

"Hey." Francesco reached for his lover's hand, but Henry put on his robe and headed back to the dining room to clean up. Francesco jumped out of bed and followed. "I love you," he said.

"Like you loved Dinky?"

"Sit down. Let's finish our wine."

Henry paused before taking his chair.

"My question was, do you love me like you loved Dinky? And really think this through before you answer."

"I love you. You're sexy."

"Give me a break." Henry rose, but this time when Francesco reached for his hand, he sat.

"You're helping me find myself again. No, really, you are. And you excite me. You know about...things, and I love listening to you. You're political —"

"I'm a blackfella. We're all political."

"And you sort me out with my ignorant views." He sipped his wine. "And you turn me on in a way I haven't felt in years. No, sit! Listen to me. Everything about you makes me feel alive..."

"Why did you stop? Surely, that's not all you have to say?"

"Okay, Henry, you want to play this game. Why are you with me?"

"Because maybe you need salvation. Maybe you need to look in the mirror and amend your ways, because quite frankly, Franky, I still can't find a solid reason why you're cheating on someone who sounds like a nice guy."

Francesco stayed deadpan. *If you only knew Stan and I share our bedroom with others.*

"I think Dinky is losing his mind," Francesco answered. "He bought a shitload of flowers the other day—"

"I know. You told me. But you started dating me long before he went all floral on you." Henry smirked at his own wordplay.

"Maybe he was Mr Right-for-now?"

"That doesn't make me Mr Right."

"You're closer to Mr Right than he is."

"For now, Franky. For now. But have you considered your man is losing it because somewhere in his mind he knows you're unfaithful?"

"Ouch."

"No, Franky, I'm serious." Henry took his lover's hands, cupping them inside his. "And I'm serious when I say I hope he's found his own sounding board. Seven-year itch. You may be both looking for clarity, just in the wrong places."

"Oh shit!" Francesco pulled his hands away from Henry's. "I'm in the wrong place."

"That's the first time you've reacted instantly to something I've said."

"Dinky's not at his mum's. Henry, what's the time?"

"I don't know. After nine?"

"I've blown it!"

"What's the matter?"

"Dinky is at the theatre alone. He planned a date. Dinner and a show."

"How could you forget?"

Francesco stood. He paced back and forth within the limited space. "Dinky and I never go out. We go to the club sometimes, but dinner and theatre is not our style. What was his motive?"

"Love? Spending time with you? He had no motive. And what do you mean, theatre is not your style? You work at a theatre. Don't you both see the plays?"

But Frank wasn't listening. He rushed back to the bedroom and gathered his clothes. He was forcing them on as he made his way to the front door. Soon he was in his car, still buttoning up his shirt. He started the engine and then turned the motor off.

He sat alone, distressed. It was too late to go to the theatre. And if he showed up it might make Stanley angrier. Besides, he wasn't sure which theatre it was. He was supposed to meet him at the restaurant and Stanley would then take him to the show.

The light had gone out in Henry's window. A set of headlights popped up from over the hill and shot past Frank's stagnant car. Another vehicle could be heard in the distance.

Francesco turned the key again. The engine purred. He drove to the restaurant where he saw a small playhouse nearby. He finally found a park. He entered the theatre.

"Hey, hold on, Mister. You can't go in without a ticket. And if you buy one, I can't let you in until interval."

Francesco felt dizzy. "Of course. I understand. Can I get a glass of water?"

"Are you all right, Mister?"

"Water. Please."

After his drink, he got into his car and went to the first place he thought of. Back to Henry's.

Chapter Twelve

Planning

"You need guidance," said Matilda, the props librarian.

She adjusted her clear-framed spectacles and gazed romantically at Asher from behind the front counter, even though she knew he didn't bat for her team.

"What are you looking for?" she asked.

"Handkerchiefs."

"Modern or retro?"

"It doesn't matter." Asher tapped his chin. "Yes, it matters. Classy."

"Then you're right. It doesn't matter. They're all classy!" She pulled out a cream-coloured card and wrote carefully between the lines.

Third row, just after tea towels and socks.

He took the card and hurried toward the third row. He stopped instinctively as he passed several stylish jackets. A burgundy one with gold stitching on its collar appealed to him. He felt its lapel. He took it from its hanger and tried it on.

"It suits you," Matilda called. "Come and check the mirror out front."

"I've always wondered..." Asher strolled back to her workspace.

"You always wondered what?"

"Why the mirror is near you and not by the costumes." He checked himself from the side and again from the front. He loved how smart he looked.

"Because every time someone tries something on, they call me over for my opinion. So, I brought the mirror here to save me from strolling down to them." She nodded, approvingly. "Who are you trying to impress?"

"No one. It's for a dream."

"I know. This is the props department, Ash. Everything here is for a dream. Now, who are you trying to impress?"

"An older man."

He stroked one of the buttons on the jacket and then glanced at her briefly, taking in her raised brow before evaluating his reflection once more.

"Yes. This is good. This is the one."

"Ash, who is he?"

"My *pro*ject." He lingered on the middle syllable.

"And you're not just trying to impress him for the end goal. I know that look. You see a future together. Down here in eternal sleep."

"No. You've got it wrong."

She marched out from behind the counter and faced him, raising her chin in an attempt to meet his eyeline.

"You can't fool me, Mr Asher with his heart on his sleeve." Matilda felt the softness of the lapel before flicking lint from his shoulder. "I've seen it all. I've seen Declan pretend his heart is stone, yet he spends ages searching for the right prop. And Baxter skips down the aisles when he thinks no one is looking. You all fall for your projects. That's why Marjorie gets annoyed. She senses it like I do. And she steers you because just like you, she has her job to do. But you can't fool me. No, none of you Midnight Men can. You fall and you fall hard." She scrunched her lips. "Have you told Marjorie?"

He shook his head.

"She's no stranger to love, you know. She advises you Midnight Men when you've fallen for your mortals all the time."

Somewhere in Matilda's words, Asher felt guilt. A truth he didn't want to share, let alone tell his instructor. The Midnight Men dutifully went to school, taking classes with Marjorie on how to help humans progress, so they wouldn't have to repeat lessons they hadn't learned in their current life into their next incarnation.

"You're contemplating." Matilda patted his hair, styling it for his date the best she could. "What's on your mind, Ash?"

"I'm about to do something really random. A dream not featured in our textbook."

She rolled her eyes. "Really? Asher, all of you flirt with your humans a little. It's not something new. It's in your textbook. It helps you win your mortals over. It's when you mistake puppy love for real love, you have a problem. Declan hurt a woman's feelings when he realised he didn't love her. And Baxter misread all the signs his man was giving him." She stepped closer and whispered, "He cried on my shoulder. His tears stained my favourite houndstooth coat."

"I'm not in love," he lied.

"Oh, yes you are. You wouldn't be doing something outside the textbook if you weren't."

Asher didn't respond.

"Do you need anything else?"

"I need the usual waiter and nice food..." He noted her expression. His words gave him away. Another date was in the making.

"I'll book the restaurant for you. Do you need a nice shirt? Tie perhaps?"

"Just a shirt and pants and..." He faced her. "And a nice coat for him."

She grinned. "You need to talk to Marjorie. She needs to know." She headed to the costume section. "Anything else?"

"Yeah. Old clothes."

"Old clothes?"

"Vagabond clothes."

"Really? What are you planning?"

"A test," he mumbled quietly to himself.

"What about the handkerchief?"

He nodded.

Matilda returned with several outfits. Asher picked the ones he wanted and then he booked extra cast members for the next dream. He bundled the clothes in his arm and hurried away.

She itemised each prop he took on his borrower's card, inscribing neatly between the flawless blue lines. Then she stared at the list, puzzled by the mixed assortment. Asher was still in her line of sight, so she sat, gazing at his cute butt and daydreaming of being the starlet in one of his dreams.

Asher stood in front of the Dream Maker Machine. Its gaping brass mouth invited his weird assortment of props. He pressed the big red button, making the appliance whir and shake. The chug of its antique engine made him step back, away from the noise. He threw the props in and covered his ears.

Sparks flew as it sucked the clothes and the handkerchief into its vortex. He pressed the chipped gold button with the word *Hotel* and then searched for the one that was marked *Homeless*. He pressed it too.

The scraping metallic sound filled him with weird joy. When Stanley was asleep again, this dream would be the deal breaker. Asher danced, springing from one foot to the next.

He imagined Stanley in his arms again. He pictured their next kiss. He envisaged a life away from Matilda's nosy musings.

Chapter Thirteen

Intensity

Stanley came home. He was glad he was alone. He splashed vodka over ice and sat on a sofa examining the purchase he'd made from the eclectic gift store next to the theatre after the play.

He opened the box. It lay on tissue paper. He carefully took it out with more care than its price warranted. He inspected it. Its aqua and purple tones dazzled him. He knocked back his vodka.

Next, he headed for the bedroom and stepped onto the bed, carefully gaining balance on the mattress. He raised the power drill steadily to the ceiling and tightened the screws that kept the hook in place. He suddenly felt the need to jump off the bed like a man half his age.

He reached for the object, hopeful and excited. Its hippy-toned feathers, a feature that would normally make him cringe, filled him with glee. He ran his finger around the circle that characterised the item. *So much work for something so ethereal.*

He stepped onto the mattress once more, his feet unsteady. He spread his arms to stay centred, moved cautiously to the middle of the bed, and hung the feature on the hook. He then lay, looking up at it with affection.

"I want to hold you, Asher, in the real world."

The dream catcher heard his words.

★

The crimson curtain surrounded Stanley and Asher once again as they sat at their table. No one else but their waiter was there. He poured wine as red as blood.

"This should warm you," the waiter said.

Stanley found reassurance in the stylish coats he and Asher were wearing.

"It's a night for comfort food," said Asher.

The waiter cleared his throat. "We have a great selection on the menu, gentlemen. But with the red you've chosen can I recommend the organic beef stew with freshly baked crusty baguettes and creamy churned butter?"

Asher's enthusiastic grin stretched into his cheeks.

"We'll both have the stew," said Stanley. He passed their unread menus to the waiter and then leaned toward Asher. "You've brought me back to the place I need to be."

"Why? What's the matter?"

"I went and saw *The Women* with my mother."

"Then why do you seem…"

"Perplexed?"

"Flummoxed."

"I was supposed to see the play with Frank. When he didn't show up to the restaurant and didn't answer my text messages, I rang Mother and asked her to the theatre."

"I told you going on a date with Franky was a bad idea."

"I wanted to share something special with him. I wanted a date to reboot us."

Asher beamed. "It seems my competition is out of the running."

Stanley didn't know how to respond. He knew he liked this romantic scenario better than his actual relationship, but he didn't see it as a competition. If only *this* relationship was real.

"Did what I say frighten you?" Asher's overconfidence delighted Stan.

"No. I enjoy feeling appreciated. And loved. I'm looking forward to our adventure tonight." He ran his fingers through his hair. "How old am I?"

"Thirty-five."

"That's a very good year," the waiter said, coming back with their wine.

"A very good year, my blue-blooded boy," Stanley whispered. "I have a feeling we rode here tonight in a limousine."

"What are you talking about?" Asher asked.

"It was a song, many years ago."

The waiter sang as he walked away. "When I was thirty-five, la de da..."

Asher shrugged. "Thirty-five was a good year for you?"

Stanley felt the lapel of his coat. "I wasn't living the high life. In fact, I've never been this rich."

He regarded Asher. The young man's burgundy jacket had an emblem stitched in gold on the upturned collar. *So Sgt. Pepper's.* His tight grey shirt accented the strong line of his chest. He could have stepped out of a fashion magazine, coming to life just long enough to tempt the reader to follow him back into the glossy pages.

"Asher, I know why I'm here."

His date nodded. "Has the real world enlightened you?"

"My mother enlightened me."

"How?" Asher observed Stanley like a student beholding a cherished mentor.

"Remember that young version of my mother you saw? She was back last night at the theatre. And we talked about you."

"You mentioned me?"

"It's the second time you came up in conversation. The first was over one of our Tuesday night dinners. She's wise, and her own love life never fails to surprise me."

Stanley swallowed hard.

"What's the matter?" Asher asked.

"Nothing."

"Darling, I can tell—"

"Darling?"

"Yes, darling..." He reached for Stan's hand. "Something's wrong."

"The odd thing is, I'm not sure what's wrong. I suddenly felt unstable but can't tell why." He shook off the feeling. "Tell me, are you going to play in a concert soon?"

"You're changing the subject."

"Trust me, I'm not."

"Yeah, soon."

"Good. Those snobby dinner guests were right about one thing. You've got to live, Asher, otherwise you'll look back on your life with regrets."

The scent of slow cooked beef interrupted Stanley's train of thought. They both looked to the waiter and the steaming clay pots on his tray. As their hearty meals were placed on the table, Asher gazed at Stanley as if he'd known him for years.

An old-fashioned meal for my old-fashioned man. Hearty, warm, and satisfying.

"I can hear your thoughts," said Stanley.

"You can?" Asher grinned as if he was about to purr.

"It's *my* dream. I'm starting to know why I come here."

They ate for a while. The caramelised carrots and tender cubes of beef melted with peppery flair on their tongues. Stanley broke the crusty bread and dipped it in his gravy. Asher did the same. They both watched each other carefully avoid getting gravy on their chins.

"So, darling, tell me about life at thirty-five."

"I was really happy at this age. I had an affair."

"You mean, a boyfriend?"

Stanley shook his head. "At the time I thought it was love, but once it was over, and it was over very quickly, I knew it was just an affair."

"He made his mark, judging by your smirk."

"Sometimes I wonder if he was the love of my life."

"But you said it was only short."

"That doesn't mean he wasn't the love of my life. There's something magic about intensity." He stared at Asher. "The sex was hot!"

"Tell me more."

"I met him when he was holidaying in Sydney. It was instant."

"Instant what?"

"Not sure. I still can't put my finger on it, but it's like you're looking at a mirror and you know the person on the other side even though you know nothing about them. He was my magnet, and I was his prey."

"That metaphor doesn't—"

"To me it makes sense. We devoured each other every moment we could. And each morning when I had to go to work, he had the bait to keep me in bed." Stanley leaned back against his chair, grinning like a demon. "We talked for hours, then had sex, then talked and had more sex. We tried every vice we could get our hands on just to make the sex more intense. It was the nineties. We had happier drugs." He slid his fingers between the buttons of his shirt, feeling his trimmer stomach under the cotton. "Hey, Asher, I'm thirty-five. Let's swap this old man stew for intensity."

Stanley tenderly rubbed his bottom lip with the tip of his finger, his mouth slightly open. Asher smiled coyly. He looked to the slightly parted curtain.

"How far would you go for love, Stanley?"

"Peel back the layers of my hardened skin and find the passion that's ready to be reborn."

"That's not the answer I expected."

Asher stood. His long coat draped over his shins, and as he walked, Stanley watched the material dance, jutting outward with each step. Asher peeled back the curtain.

"Where are we going?" Stanley asked.

"To find intensity."

A neon sign lit the darkness on the other side of the curtain. Each letter flashed individually until all stayed bright. They spelled *Hotel*.

Handsome doormen opened car doors for socialites too overdressed for daily life. A small boy tested his luck on the glass revolving door, running in just as it opened and running out before it was no longer possible. A white limousine pulled up to wait for a glamorous guest.

"Let's check into the hotel, Asher. The penthouse suite, perhaps?"

"No. Let's take this car and make love in the back seat."

But another version of Stanley and Asher climbed into the white limousine. The real Stanley looked down at his clothes. His chic black coat was now a rugged denim jacket, torn in several places. To his side was Asher. He had a beard, knotted and grubby, and a dirty scratch on his forehead. Stanley caught another glimpse of the other version of themselves riding away. They were kissing intensely.

"It's cold," said Asher.

Stanley wrapped his arms around the young man, nestling him into his body. Their stomachs grumbled, and Stan was feeling faint.

"This doesn't make sense, Ash. We just ate."

"No, we didn't." Asher pointed at the car that was nearly out of sight. "*They* just ate."

Stan shivered. His breath turned to mist as it left his lips.

"We need to find shelter," said Asher.

A car shot past, splashing water from a puddle onto their already muddy clothes.

"It doesn't look like it's been raining," said Stanley. "Where did that—"

"Quick, darling, I need food."

They staggered. Asher huddled close to Stan's chest. They passed a garbage bin and Stanley picked something red from near the top, thinking it was food. He dropped it in horror the moment its form became clear. But his need to sneeze overpowered the disgust he would normally feel from this bloodied handkerchief. He picked it up and held it near his face. The contents of his nose added abstract colour to its crimson canvas.

"It's not normal!" yelled a voice behind them.

Stanley was too scared to look. His hands shot into his threadbare pockets, sinking the bloodied cloth deep inside. Somehow this act gave him security.

"Poverty! We're the sewerage of noblemen." A short grungy guy tottered past. He continued muttering more words to anyone prepared to listen.

"Where can we get food?" Asher called to the moaning man.

The grungy stranger stopped. "Soup." He pointed. "That way."

Soon Stan and Ash found a charity van and sat with other homeless men slurping their handouts.

"How much to sleep with your tender plaything?"

Stanley could not believe what he'd heard.

"I have cigarettes. One in exchange for your boy."

He ignored the repulsive request. Then an elbow slammed into his gut. His soup launched into the air and splashed on the footpath. He grabbed the adherent man's bowl and hit him across the face with it. He then brought it down on his skull to accentuate his point.

"That's my friend you've attacked!" cried another creepy guy who lisped due to his lack of teeth. He grabbed Asher and licked his cheek, slobbering like a mutt. "We share our treasures 'round here."

Stanley lunged forward, throwing a punch, but his wayward aim missed its target. Instead, he caught a blow to his jaw and hit the ground. But through his agony he stood and charged into the disgusting man. He bowled him over, taking Asher to the ground with him. The man grabbed at Asher's jeans, trying to reach for the zipper, but Stanley wrapped his hand around the man's throat and squeezed until the deadbeat gasped in desperation. As his eyes bulged, Stan let go and slapped the man's face for good measure.

A stream of water now washed away Stanley's anger, but it wasn't rain. He was showering with Asher in the largest en suite he had ever seen.

"Ash, why did we go through all that drama?"

"Intensity. Would you have gone this far to protect Franky? Or even that 'love of your life' affair guy?"

"I wouldn't go this far for Franky. Not now."

A gentle snore could be heard from the bedroom. Francesco and Stanley, both in the early stages of their relationship, were nestled together, sleeping soundly under the sheets in full view from the shower.

"Oh my..." Stanley gazed at their former selves. "There was a time I'd have done anything for Franky."

Francesco subconsciously moved to spoon Stan as they slept.

"You just saved me from those creeps, and you just said you'd probably do the same for Franky—"

"I said there was a *time* I would have done the same for Franky."

"So, do you know what love is?"

Stanley's gut churned. Soon he was sobbing.

"No need to reply," said Asher. "I know the answer."

Stanley woke. Francesco snored beside him. Asher's words swam around his head like a goldfish looking for a way out of its bowl.

The more he thought about the strange dream, the more confused he was. He sat up, quickly, not understanding his haste. He stepped out of bed and strode to the laundry where he found underwear, socks, and a T-shirt he'd worn in the last few days. He went back to the bedroom and quietly picked a clean pair of jeans and a jacket from the wardrobe.

His keys were gripped carefully so they wouldn't make a sound, and with purpose, Stanley made his way into the street.

Do I know love? Who have I loved? Who am I in love with?

Francesco's caring face, the one Stanley knew well when they'd first met, came to mind. Stan felt a weird concoction of love and loss. He could feel Franky's touch; that gentle rub to Stan's palm he used to do while they talked in bed. The caress to Stan's neck that helped put him to sleep in their early years.

He saw the long coat in the shop window he'd fallen in love with several days before. He stopped briefly to admire it. The weird dream replayed in his head, but this time he imagined Asher and himself wearing some of the other swanky fashion from this store, instead of the jackets they wore at dinner.

I want to spoil him. I want to show him off and say, "he's mine". I want to tell people "He brings me to life!" Why can't he be real?

Stanley moved on, heading straight into the laneway where he'd previously run from a homeless man. There was no fear this time as he stepped into the darkness. He made out the man's face peering into the night, his back against the bricks. Stan reached for his wallet and took out two hundred dollars. He grabbed the man's greasy hand and planted the money in his palm.

The man stayed silent. He studied Stanley's expression. Kindness. Nothing more than kindness. The man clasped the cash and cried.

Stan walked away, his hands snugly nestled in the pockets of his jacket.

What is this?

He pulled at what was inside his left pocket and casually brought it to his face. Its colour was intense under the harsh streetlights.

Huh?

There it was between his fingers, red and wet. The bloodied handkerchief.

Chapter Fourteen

Charity

"Welcome to giving up your nights in front of the TV," said Henry. He shook Stanley's hand. "So, what brought you here?"

"I'm not sure. Gut feeling? I've been driven to do a lot of things lately I can't explain."

Henry gave him an odd stare while Stanley scanned the room. Homeless people of all shapes, sizes, and colours were tottering in. Some held their worldly possessions in plastic bags while one pushed a battered shopping cart.

"That's where you'll be stationed," Henry said. He pointed to another volunteer in the kitchen cooking dinner for the disenfranchised. "Come with me."

Stanley followed his supervisor. He was given a hair net and an apron which he put on instantly to show his keenness. An introduction to the other helper was made and soon Stanley was dishing out steamed rice onto plates with the efficiency of a worker on an assembly line. Henry took each plate and added curried chicken before handing it to the hungry waiting in line. This routine went on for fifteen minutes before the rush quietened down. The cook took this opportunity to pop outside and drag on a cigarette.

"That one, over there," said Stanley, gesturing discreetly to a blond man wolfing his food down. "Forgive me if I'm stereotyping, but he seems too young to be homeless."

"You mean, too good looking?"

"Perhaps."

"Yeah, I noticed you had your eye on him."

"Who is he, Henry?"

"We call him Billy, but we don't know his real name."

"Why don't you ask him?"

"He doesn't talk. Some of the others told us he's returned from a tour of duty. Whatever horrors he's seen silenced him."

Stanley watched Billy eat. Every time his fork came near his mouth, he paused and stared at the food skewered in its prongs. Then he carefully placed the curry in his mouth before pulling the fork out steadily. Stan grabbed a tablespoon, marched over, and offered it to Billy.

The young man took it gracefully and then held the fork high in the air, looking away from it as if it was a weapon to be wary of. Stanley extracted the malevolent cutlery from his hand and brought it back to the kitchen.

"How does someone break through to him?" Stanley asked. "How does someone love him?"

"The real question is, how does *he* learn to love again?"

"Where are his parents?"

"They probably keep an eye on him from a distance. He might have terrorised them in their home. There're a million reasons why these people are here. See the man in the suit hardly touching his food?"

"The one with scratches on his cheek?"

"Yep. Doctor."

"What?"

"He's a doctor."

Stanley didn't know how to respond. Various questions darted through his head before he quietly mumbled, "Why?"

"It took some time, but we finally worked it out when the police verified he was a missing person. His kids reported him gone and when we checked the online records, he matched the description."

"But he's a doctor?"

"He can't remember his past. You see, when his wife died it was too much for him. He locked his house up and left. He hasn't returned for two years."

"Imagine a love so strong that you lose your mind once it's over."

"You say that with longing, Stanley. Are you looking for a boyfriend?"

"Oh, Henry, I'm not single but…"

Stanley observed the widower and the serviceman as if no one else was in the room. He tried to imagine what the wife of the doctor was like. Vivacious, maybe? Jolly, perhaps? Someone who left her mark for life, which had now become his life sentence.

The serviceman seemed at ease with his spoon. And while the doctor once met his true love, the soldier might never be ready to meet his soulmate. The perfect woman might now be on a different path, the gods guiding her to calmer waters.

"Asher," Stanley mumbled.

"Is that your boyfriend's name?" Henry asked.

"Sorry, I didn't mean to say anything then."

"I won't be nosy." Henry checked the pot of curry. "Whatever is left you can take home."

"Thanks. And hey, you weren't being nosy." Stanley smirked. "My lover's name is Asher."

"Lover? Not partner or boyfriend?"

"I think it's an affair. It won't last but it's intense. And boy, he makes me feel *good*."

"Well, if he's rockin' your boat, it doesn't matter who he is." Henry smirked.

"I'm sure you'll find someone someday."

"Stanley, I'm having an affair too."

"Good on you!" Stan shot his palm into the air and high-fived his new friend. "What's his name?"

"Ah, I can't say. I've got to keep it secret."

"Why? Is he in the closet?"

"Something like that, and you know how us old queens like to gossip."

"You can trust me, Henry."

"I'm sure I can. I promise to tell you during our next shift. I just need to know you better. You understand?"

"I understand perfectly." Stanley saw Asher's youthful smile in his mind. "What is it about an affair that makes it so perfect?"

"Perfect? Mine is far from perfect."

"Why?"

"Keeping a relationship secret is no fun." Henry turned the temperature down on the curry. "I envy you, Stan. It sounds like your affair is keeping you young."

"It's doing more than that. It's making me reassess."

"Reassess?"

"Reassess my life. My choices." He laughed to himself. "My demons."

"In a good way, I hope."

"Yes, Henry. In a good way."

"Go on."

"In his own way, Asher is unattainable." Stanley laughed to himself again. "I mean, I know it won't last. It can't. But Asher is helping me see myself in a different light. I'm actually starting to like myself again."

"That's what an affair is supposed to do. Why won't it last?"

"Affairs never last. We learn. We move on. And the fact that I recognise it as just an affair means I'm being more honest with myself than usual." Stanley paused for a moment. "So, Henry, tell me about your affair? What are you getting out of it?"

"Perspective. That's what I seem to get from all my affairs, perspective. I seem to attract men who need a reality check and at the same time, I learn from their mistakes. They move on. They always move on. Then I'm left with insight on how to treat Mr Right, whenever he's destined to finally come along."

"How will you know it's Mr Right?"

"When he's not trying to find himself!"

The cook re-entered the shelter. Stanley smelt nicotine.

"And what's your love life like?" Stanley asked.

"I don't believe in love," the cook replied. "You see, love lingers like a virus."

"There's a perspective we hadn't considered," Stanley said to Henry.

"It sounds like we're all on a different page," Henry replied.

"Well, here's to the three of us…" Stanley stood at the fridge checking its contents. He pulled out a carton of orange juice and filled three glasses. "Like I said, here's to the three of us at different stages of life. And to the lovers helping us along the way!"

Chapter Fifteen

Eternity

"Am I thirty, Ash?"

"Yes, you are. Lucky guess."

"I'd call it an educated guess."

Asher was driving again in his sports car. Stanley was disappointed that this dream didn't begin with dinner, but as they passed the familiar terrace houses, he feared he'd be dining once more with the people who'd deemed him unworthy.

"I can sense your unease, darling," said Asher.

"Yeah..." Stanley placed his hand on the young man's knee. "But I'm invincible because I have you by my side."

Asher sat straighter, leading with his chest. "So, darling, what was thirty like?"

"They were my dark years. I went through an emo phase."

"You? Emo?" Ash glimpsed at Stan twice. "Actually, at thirty you'd look good as an emo."

Stanley pulled down his sun visor. It had a mirror. "My hair was darker than it is now. And the black lipstick only came out for concerts. Pub concerts, mainly."

"Like this one?" Asher planted a seed to allow Stanley to guide the dream.

They were no longer in the car. The band in front of them had their speakers at ear-splitting levels. Their thrash metal drumbeat echoed from the cracked walls. Everywhere Asher looked, black was in vogue. Clothes. Lipstick. Eyeliner. Nail polish.

Stanley joined the others in jumping on the spot.

"What are you doing?" Asher asked.

"Dancing."

"On a pogo stick?"

"Try it."

Asher did. His laughter became infectious and soon Stanley giggled at his own carefree act.

"Why is no one smiling?" Asher shouted.

"It's called *I take life too seriously*. Also known as youth."

The guitarists battled for dominance. The drummer's sweat sprayed outward like a sprinkler every time he moved his head to the beat. The singer growled more than he sang, barking random words in the improvised art-rock piece.

Some of the crowd pumped their fists forward, calling back random words of their own. One stumbled into Asher before bouncing away like a ball struck in a pinball machine. He toppled onto a stoned woman. She fell to the ground. Her friend tugged on her arm but struggled to get her back on her feet.

Fog, with a weird chemical odour, dispensed into the mob. Its hazy wayward form was tinted by primary-coloured lights. Asher coughed.

Stanley took Asher's hand and led him to the back of the bar. There were several musty smelling booths which were large enough to sit groups of friends. Stan found one where a girl and guy were kissing, unaware that their space was about to be invaded. Stanley sat at the edge of the bench. He moved in slightly to give Asher room. He took Asher's jaw and turned his lips toward his. Asher closed his eyes and let Stanley love him.

Dark lipstick smeared on Asher's mouth, like crayon. He didn't mind. Its oily feel added lubrication to this kiss. Its bland taste made Stanley's energetic odour more noticeable. The crazed tunes and the crazed crowd gave Asher a sense of adolescence he'd never felt. An appreciation of the chaos. A lust for life.

Time passed. Stanley never kissed anyone nearly ten years younger, and he didn't feel the sum of his forty-nine years. This thirty-year-old emo was not brooding on the decline of civilisation or the evils of capitalism. He was lost in his dreams with someone who loved him back.

"This is not what I planned," Asher yelled over the music.

"After what happened in my last dream, I think I prefer this."

"Come." Asher moved forward in the seat. "Take one last look at this scene."

The audience leaped around like popcorn in a microwave. Some crashed into others. One guitarist was cemented to his spot while the other joined the singer at the front of the stage. They yelled at the crowd, ignoring the microphone.

"Thank you for this, Asher."

With this cue, the Midnight Man took back control of this dream. Stanley was back in the car, admiring himself in the mirror.

"I like visiting your past. I liked seeing you as a boy with your mum. And I liked seeing that black-lipstick-wearing Stan in his natural environment."

"Did you like being kissed by that Stan?"

"That goes without saying."

They arrived at the brass gates of the well-known house. Stan stopped admiring his younger self.

"Have you travelled yet?" asked the woman as she answered the door. She wore the same red dress from the other dreams. "I mean, the painted fingernails and the eyeliner are very Euro. You must have travelled."

"I'm travelling in a different way," Stanley replied. He entered, leading Asher by the hand.

"Oh, it's you!" the man with peppered curly hair exclaimed. He turned to the hostess who was still at the front door. "I knew we had a couple of mystery guests, but I never imagined you meant Asher and..." He snapped his fingers several times in the air. "...Mark?"

"Stanley," Ash replied.

They sat at the table still holding hands.

"I don't believe you told me your names the last time we were here," said Stan.

"Do you ever know all the characters in your dreams?" the man with the bowtie asked. "And even when you do, do you remember their names by the time you wake?"

"What a dull conversation," said the woman. She joined them at the dining table. "Now tell me, Asher, how's your flute playing? Will you be joining us on stage soon?"

"I'll be joining your orchestra in two more dreams."

"Splendid!" She turned to Stanley. "You look younger. You remind me of Richard."

"Who's Richard?"

"You remember, my lover in Prague."

"Wasn't that Robert?"

"Oh, sweetheart, I've had so many lovers I lose track of their names."

She gave Stanley a stern look. In turn, he gave Asher a curious look.

"I *never* forget their names," said the curly-haired one. "Even if it's a quickie." He gestured vaguely. "I mean, you never know when you might meet again."

Stanley wanted to roll his eyes but kept control. A lovely young woman in a black uniform and sheer stockings entered the dining room. She placed a silver serving tray with a lid on the table.

"What are we eating tonight?" Stan asked her.

"Oh, we don't fraternise with the staff," said the man with the bowtie.

Stanley felt unease. "Why not?" His tone was measured.

"Well, they're the *staff.*"

"Excuse their rudeness, Madam, but what are we eating tonight?" Stan asked again.

She lifted the lid. A pie in a baking tin sat next to a small gravy boat.

"You're dismissed," the hostess uttered, her manner curt.

The maid curtsied and then stepped backward toward the door through which she entered.

"I didn't catch your name," said Stanley. She stopped, looking as nervous as a lamb in an abattoir. "Don't mind them, my dear. Ash and I were *brought* up, not *dragged* up like the others in this room."

"Well, I never!" cried the hostess.

"Never what? Never missed the chance to sleep with any man who crossed your path?"

"That was uncalled for. You simply don't understand social norms."

"Seriously? That's your comeback. You and your friend just insulted the young woman who works for you, and you think it's acceptable. You didn't think someone would pull you up on your bad behaviour?"

"My bad behaviour? *My* bad behaviour?" She pulled at her tight-fitting dress as if loosening it to let off steam. "My staff are my staff. How I talk to them is my business.

And it's not up to my guests to point out how I should address them. I have class!"

"Not at this moment, you don't. You've never had to work for a living. You've never had the empathy to understand those in need. And although you've fucked every man who showed interest, it never caused you to develop character."

"Character! I have more character in the tip of my finger than you have in your entire body."

Stanley stood. "Your inflated sense of self-importance proves otherwise."

"That's a bit strong," said the curly-haired man, only half audible.

"I don't think so. I think I used the same amount of respect she showed the lovely woman who brought us pie." Asher stood and took Stanley's hand. He squeezed it in an approving manner. Stan grinned at the maid who was also smiling. "What is your name?"

"Magda."

"Hello, Magda. I'm Stanley and this here is Asher. The rest, well, are they worthy of an introduction?"

She leaned forward. "I don't think so." She faced her employer. "As for you, Mrs Worthington, the potatoes are already boiled and just need mashing. You do know how to mash a potato, don't you?"

The hostess grumbled. The maid headed for the front door.

"Don't forget, I own that uniform you're wearing!"

Her former employee stopped, stripped, and let her clothes fall to the floor. She slammed the door on the way out.

"Well, Mrs Worthington, go mash the potatoes," Stanley said. "Anyone care to join me for a joint in the garden?"

"I didn't know you smoked dope." Asher wore an eager grin.

"Hey. It's my dream."

★

"Have I ruined your chance at playing flute in their orchestra?" Stanley asked Asher. He passed the spliff to him.

"In dreamland, any scenario can be rewritten." Asher kissed Stanley on the cheek. "I'm so proud of you."

"No one should be bullied. And it's our duty to make sure no one ever is."

"Intriguing."

"What's intriguing?"

"Darling, were you ever bullied?"

Stanley was about to reply that he wasn't, but those words caught in his throat. Instead, he looked back at the house. The lights were on and the table still had the serving tray with the steaming pie waiting to be eaten, but neither the hostess nor the other guests could be seen.

"Where are they, Ash?"

"Where all fantasy characters go until they're needed again."

"And where's that?"

Asher looked as if he was about to reveal the meaning of life.

"Into limbo," he replied.

Stanley breathed in the answer. "I've never felt younger, or as rebellious, as I do now."

"Does that worry you?"

"It shouldn't, but it does." Stan dragged on the joint, sucking like an exhaust fan and exhaling smoke rings into the night. "Usually, I'd be nervous. But I'm not. I'm playing against type because here with you, I'm a superhero. I'm invincible. I'm Stanley." He sighed. "Asher, why do you love me? Before you answer that I want you to understand that you said some weird things about love the last time we met. I'm scared that any moment we'll be homeless again."

Asher chuckled. "What did I say that you thought was weird?"

"A whole jumble of things about intensity, and the intensity in which we love."

"So, what do you really want to know, Stan? My meaning of intensity or why I love you?"

"Do both questions have the same answer?"

"I'm not sure. I love you because every time I see you, you come to life more."

"Why? Was I dead?"

"You were, in a way. But I keep seeing new facets of my mystery man."

"Asher, how old are you, really? Are you older than the body you inhabit?"

"No. I've just been guided by smart people."

"And do you always fall in love with those you're helping?"

Asher avoided the question. He guided Stanley onto the grass. They laid back.

"You're special," Asher finally replied.

"Am I special just because you've seen my younger selves?"

"Your older self is just as sexy as the other versions."

The ground felt more like luxurious carpet than wet lawn. Asher eased himself on top of his lover and caressed his jaw.

"At thirty I still had good bone structure," Stanley said.

Ash pressed his cheek against Stan's, rubbing the small amount of stubble he had into Stan's skin. *Frisky,* Stan thought. He went to kiss his younger lover, but Asher placed his finger on Stanley's lips.

"There's intensity in true love," said Asher.

"You see, again I feel you're saying something but not saying something..."

Ash slid the erection housed in his jeans against Stan's groin. Stan moaned. He could feel his own starting to stir. Ash grinned like the naughtiest Playboy bunny in the mansion. He puckered his lips and blew gently onto Stan's face. Stan felt the air push against his thick head of hair, so he closed his eyes and waited for a kiss.

"Come with me, Stanley," Ash whispered. "Slip with me into eternal sleep."

"That sounds both romantic and sinister. Do you honestly love me?"

"Of course, I do. The question is, do you love me?"

"At this point in time, Asher, I'm falling deeper than I ever have. I'm young—"

"You were never old, Stanley."

Stan laughed absurdly. "Sh. Ash, don't spoil this moment. I'm invincible tonight. I'm young and I have someone who inspires me." He remembered the scene with himself and Francesco in the bath and how he was told he inspired Francesco. It all made sense.

"Asher, I do love you. You bring out the best in me."

"So, fall with me into eternal sleep."

With his eyes still closed, Stanley felt one soft kiss before the dream faded.

Chapter Sixteen

Circus

Francesco sat on a rickety wooden chair, his back pressed hard against the support. All he could think of was how aware he was of his spine, until he saw them. Two very composed butlers walking down the aisles, holding silver serving trays. One balanced three ritzy champagne flutes on his platter while clasping a bottle of sparkling wine in his other hand. The second butler had a pair of scarlet gloves and opera glasses on his tray. Between them were several rows of those uncomfortable chairs seating a multitude of very average looking families.

The waiters shuffled down the steps on both sides of the raked seating until they were nearly at the bottom. When they stopped, both bent over and reached toward a woman in a red dress. *She's definitely not average*, Francesco thought.

Next to her sat two men, one with distinct peppered hair as curly as ramen noodles. The other wore a jacket and bowtie.

An elephant roared. Francesco became aware of the animal tamer who stood in the ring surrounded by the crowd. The elephant roared again but somehow the woman in red and her companions were not interested in the show. She was using her glasses to spy on someone in the audience.

Francesco turned and grinned when he saw who caught her attention. It was Stanley seated some distance away. At least, it looked like Stanley. *Why is he so young?*

This was a version of his partner he'd only seen in photos. The twentysomething in a waistcoat and T-shirt, and hair sculpted with so much gel it resembled the rough end of a pineapple. To Francesco this 1980s fashion victim was adorable. He thought how nice it would have been to know Stanley then. To be caught up in love in seemingly endless youth.

A young man next to Stan was talking to him as if they knew each other well. He played with Stanley's hair before wrapping his arms around Stanley's shoulders. This guy was not an eighties throwback. He was the boy next door. The type Francesco masturbated to many times while admiring his teen sister's pop magazines. If only she understood why her choice of reading material kept disappearing.

Stanley gazed at the enigmatic man in a way Francesco remembered well. The look of love that used to be bestowed on him many years before.

The men kissed. Lips locked like lovers who were in for the long haul.

Francesco gradually looked away; the blurred image of the audience and the elephant standing on its hind legs whizzed past with no significance. A sadness he couldn't comprehend pushed down on him. Stanley was not *his* back then. Perhaps in years to come he never would be. This cute young man would steal him long before the day Francesco and Dinky were destined to meet.

Francesco felt it in the pit of his stomach. Something anguished. Something vocal. As the elephant roared again, he, too, hollered for understanding. But no one listened. No one cared. His dream faded to black as his cry lingered in the darkness.

"I'm twenty-five, aren't I?" Stanley asked as he ran his fingers through the sharp points of his own hair.

"Yes, you are," Asher replied.

"I don't remember going to the circus when I was twenty-five."

"So, we're making new memories."

Asher reached for a glass of champagne on a waiter's tray. He passed it to Stanley and reached for another.

"Mother took me to the circus when I was young, but I don't remember alcohol being served. It's a shame. Mother likes to drink."

They clinked glasses.

An elephant roared as it stood on its hind legs. Its tamer chucked an oversized ball into the air which the elephant bounced on its trunk before balancing it steadily.

"What's the matter, Asher? What are you looking at?"

"Ever get that feeling you're being...yeah, we are being watched." He pointed.

The woman in the red dress was spying on them through opera glasses. Asher waved, surprised she and her friends made their way to this dream. Her two companions waved back.

"Why are they so interested in us?" Stanley asked.

"Because we're happier than they are."

"You know your friends well, if they really are your friends."

"They're a means to an end."

"Well, I hope after you play in their orchestra, you'll find some 'down to earth' musicians. Like a fusion rock band that needs a flute player."

"Or a punk band that needs a flautist for their emo audience."

"A punk band with a flautist?"

"Yeah!" Asher raised his glass. "A toast to cool musicians."

The elephant roared again. Three clowns ran into the ring and danced like uncoiled springs around the animal. One pulled out a harmonica and played a number neither Stanley nor Asher recognised. It sounded like a forgotten nursery rhyme. Next, an organ grinder entered and accompanied the lost tune.

"This whole scene feels eerie," Stanley noted.

"Maybe we should find something a twenty-five-year-old and a twenty-one-year-old would rather do?" Asher put his glass on the ground and felt his lover's gel-stiffened hair.

"Careful, you'll mess with its youthful rebellious abandon."

"I'm sure there are other ways to be youthful, or rebellious, or..."

He wrapped his arms around Stanley's shoulders and eased him to his lips. They kissed. The anarchic melody weaved into the background, faint and unobtrusive.

Stanley lost himself. A man in his twenties kissing a man in his twenties. Smooth tight lips exploring smooth tight lips. Tongues ravishing. Endless paths with endless possibilities for love to sprout like a well-watered garden.

Asher was equally lost with a man just four years older. A little wiser than himself. Skin a little tighter than the previous versions of his dreamer. Libido more reckless. Spontaneity replacing melancholy.

Asher kissed Stanley's earlobe. "I know a place," he whispered.

He walked him out of the circus tent. A few stalls were littered around the lawn outside. Asher stopped leading Stanley, pausing in front of a stand which offered a luscious childhood treat. A plump woman in a headscarf picked two of the delicacies by their sticks and handed them to the lovers.

Asher bit into the shell of his, cracking the toffee with a discernible crunch. Soon the soft apple inside rewarded him with sweet juice.

Stanley smelt his. Its hard sugar casing had to be experienced, not just eaten. This was a delight his mother rewarded him with when they visited the circus. He licked the sweet, his tongue melting the sticky outer layer. It made biting it so much softer.

They held hands and left the toffee apple stand.

"Where are we, Asher?"

"At the circus."

"No. We were at the circus. Where did everything go?"

"I took you to the circus, but it's *your* dream. *You* brought us here."

"Why?"

"You tell me."

The alleyway the homeless man lived in was back. But at first, they couldn't see him. At the other end was sub-dued light where another figure stood in the shadows. He stepped forward but his face remained hidden. His uniform, however, had not.

And although there was limited light, the navy colour of his outfit was distinct. His brimmed hat sported a chequered pattern around its centre, while a shiny metal badge somehow reflected light back into the alley—right onto the face of the homeless man. He sat, anguished. Stanley stepped forward with false bravado as the drifter mouthed the word "Go!"

That odd melody played by the clown and the organ grinder returned. The lovers were seated again inside the tent. The elephant watched Stanley with sad eyes.

Welcome to my nightmare, Stan thought.

"I can hear you thinking," said Asher. "We should leave. Promise me that your mind won't go wandering and bring us back here, or to that alley."

Stanley admired Asher, even through his own concerns. He led Asher out of the tent. Again, the scarfed woman offered the men toffee apples.

"No thanks," said Stanley. "We just ate."

There were more stalls than before. Jugglers, snake charmers, and fire breathers added to the surreal landscape. Poetry was being recited here and there by those touched with a sense of amateur dramatics, while the sound of someone signing opera added a unique soundtrack to this scene.

"This is much better, Stanley. You feel safe, so I feel safe."

Asher reached for his lover's cheek, caressed it, and brought his lips to Stanley's. They kissed once more. Stan tried to take more comfort in Asher's affection than before, because the truth was, he didn't feel safe. He had to get lost in this kiss. The man in uniform unnerved him, yet there was no reason for his haunted feeling.

"Come," said Asher.

He led his dreamer into another tent. Asher zipped it shut and then attached a padlock through the pull tab and the metal ring sewn into a flap. No one could enter.

Stanley and Francesco's bed was inside, with the same bedside drawers and the same dream catcher hanging above.

Stan embraced the thought of making love with Asher in his own bed. He was surprised by his lack of guilt. It didn't even feel like Francesco existed, well, not yet anyway. Franky wouldn't enter his life for another seventeen years. The more he looked at Asher, the more this didn't feel like cheating.

The horny young men with too much energy to spare hastily undressed, helping each other rip off fiddly belts and pull down fussy jeans. They licked every part of each other, a taste test full of surprises.

Stanley felt there was not a care in the world. And Asher felt a connection he wanted to take further. One had forgotten what it was like to feel young with so much to discover, while the other couldn't wait for the years, and the wisdom that came with them, to accumulate like treasured possessions. And both were feeling new, waiting to be spoiled.

Stanley moved his focus upward, steadily, until he was staring at the dream catcher. He concentrated, willing this dream into the mystical object.

★

"Am I losing you?" Francesco whispered.

He'd just woken from his circus dream. Stanley was sleeping soundly, smiling in silent thought. Francesco got out of bed and fumbled for his slippers.

The night sky was odd. The moon was muted by the clouds that rolled quickly past, yet the trees in the front garden weren't rustling. For some reason, cats were loitering on the front lawn.

Francesco stopped peering at the surreal landscape, deciding instead to warm some milk.

Toffee apples?

He stared at the half dozen treats in the fridge. He remembered putting away leftovers before bedtime but didn't recall toffee apples on the middle shelf. All of a sudden, he didn't feel like warm milk. He felt spooked.

He marched quickly back to bed, but lay awake, pondering what late night market was nearby and when did Stanley go out to buy toffee apples.

Chapter Seventeen

Rekindling

The next morning, Stanley ambled down the stairs, light footed. That's the way Francesco perceived his partner as he cracked eggs into a bowl.

"Scrambled?" he asked Stan.

"But you can't cook!"

"I'm learning."

"Are you still on your guilt trip, Franky?"

"A little."

"I already told you I forgive you. I had a great time at the theatre with Mother."

"But that's not the point. I should have been there."

"There's only so many times I can listen to you apologise. And yes, I'd like my eggs scrambled with a touch of pepper."

Francesco whisked a little milk in with the eggs. The oil in the pan was already sizzling so Stanley turned down the heat before reaching for the bread bin. Then he realised the toaster was already crisping four sourdough slices.

"You're glowing, Dinky."

"Is that a good thing?"

"It's not a bad thing. You seem younger without being younger if that makes sense."

"You mean I have a spring in my step."

"That too."

Francesco took the bowl and poured the frothy liquid into the pan. The eggs took form. He soon scooped the fluffy fare onto their plates.

"This is nice," he said.

"What? Breakfast?"

"Breakfast together."

Stanley grinned but not because of what his partner said. He was thinking about Asher.

"There! You're glowing again, Dinky."

Francesco shook his tush as he placed the plates on the dining table. He turned to face Stan who wasn't paying attention to either him or his words. Stanley was at the kitchen bench swirling the butter over the toast with the knife, as if he was tracing a road on a map. "Yeah," he half sang. But this phrase had no meaning other than a sound for contentment.

He's at one with himself, Francesco thought. In this relaxed form Stanley was someone else. Someone Francesco hadn't seen since he cherished Stanley with pure love many years before. Dinky was perfect in this moment. *Calm. And glowing. Yes, glowing.*

Stanley gave his partner a reliable smile. "Breakfast at the dining table? So, if this isn't about our date at the theatre, is it our anniversary or something?"

"Why are you so...you?"

"Because I can't be someone else." He chuckled, making his way to the table. "Why are you fascinated with me today, Franky?"

"I don't know. When was the last time I told you you were beautiful?"

"Have you got a fever?"

"No, I mean it. You're special."

Stanley gave a blank stare before seating himself and trying his first mouthful of egg. "Not bad. A bit too oily, but other than that, not bad." He crunched his toast. The rich butter coated his tongue. "So, Franky, why did you cook breakfast?"

"Because I want to spoil you."

"No, Franky. I've known you too long to believe that one day you woke up and wanted to spoil me. What have you done?"

"You're so suspicious, Dinky."

"No. I'm a realist. Should we have champagne with our breakfast? Will that make you tell me the truth?" Stanley headed for the fridge to see if there was bubbly. There wasn't. "Can you drink martini with eggs?"

"Sit down, Dink. There is no hidden motive behind breakfast this morning. It's just that there's an old you lurking around and I'm finding it charming."

"An old me? You mean a nearly fifty-year-old me." Stanley sat, chewing slowly.

"No. I mean an earlier version of you in our home lately. A happier you. A sexier..." Francesco stopped himself. They hadn't made love in two weeks, and he didn't want to allude to it. "You're your old self."

"Frank, are you having an affair?"

"No!" He quickly calmed himself from his initial overreaction. "We share other bed partners so why would I need an affair? Are you having an affair?"

Stanley didn't answer. To his own surprise, he felt composed. He had the upper hand.

"Of course, you're not having an affair. Sorry, Dinky."

"Did you really think I was having an affair, or did you just ask because I asked?"

"No, I asked because you seem like your old self."

"My old self? We've hardly seen each other in the past week, and when we have, we haven't talked."

"We talked!"

"Polite conversation. 'How was your day?' 'Fine, thank you.' 'Oh look, Avril's done her hair.' 'I don't know Avril.' Our usual isolated banter in between talking to others on our own social media streams."

"Is it wrong of me to try to do something about our lack of connection?" Francesco watched Stanley attempt a smile. "I meant what I said, Dink. You're rekindling something in me. You may be turning fifty, but the clock is turning you back to your reflective self. Don't think I didn't notice the dream catcher above our bed. That's something my old Stanley would do."

Right now, Stanley didn't feel like the old Stanley. He felt like a new Stanley even as questions were plaguing him. *Has that himbo left you, Franky? And are you scared of being alone?* He eased back in his chair, toast still in hand, and changed the subject.

"I apologised to Tony and Graham. And Lucy and Nathan and Elliot as well. All of them were in the pub."

"I know. You've told me about it."

"I know I have, but I still can't get over how nice they are. Even Elliot. He had 'tude, but he was nice."

"Graham told me you looked as nervous as a virgin in a brothel."

"It was too late to turn back after I saw Lucy and her friends. Trust me, I wanted to run, but with five pairs of eyes on me there was only one way forward."

Stanley paused, not wanting to bore Francesco with a conversation they'd already had.

"They're a good bunch of people," said Francesco. "Solid friends."

"Yeah. And I know I said it before, but they made me feel like part of their gang." Stan frowned and then perked up again, taking in a mouthful of egg.

"What's the matter?" Francesco asked.

"I can't tell you."

"Why not?"

"It's stupid."

"They accepted your apology. What was stupid?"

"It wasn't Tony or Graham or the others. It was..."

"Go on."

Stanley centred himself. A deep breath in and a slow exhale. "I didn't tell you this because I'm not sure why I felt like this. I got distracted after I left them and found myself next to a homeless man in an alley…"

"Go on, Dinky."

"And I was scared."

"Of the homeless man?"

"No. The thing is I wasn't sure why I was scared." He stared at his eggs. "No. I do know why I was scared." He ran his fork along the edge of his plate.

"Dinky, go on."

"You see, I do know but I don't know. I've been scared like that before, Franky. Decades ago. And no, not from a homeless man. I was in an alley. That's all I remember. Except for a policeman."

Another deep breath. Another slow exhale. Then another inhale.

"Dinky, don't think about it. Your worry lines aren't pretty."

"Thanks. I'm facing fifty and now you're telling me I look—"

"Stan, you're as beautiful now as the day I met you."

"I still think there's a motive behind these compliments. And I think you're still feeling guilty about missing our date." He studied Francesco, wondering if this was the version who once doubted the colour of the paint or spooned him with unending affection. "Let's cook breakfast together more often. It's nice to just talk."

"I agree."

Stanley noted Francesco's sudden bewildered expression. "What is it?"

Frank strolled to the fridge, opened it, shook his head, and then closed the door. "Dinky."

"Yes?"

"Did you buy toffee apples?"

Chapter Eighteen

Concern

Asher's flute playing reverberated from the cement walls, giving church organ grandeur to his notes. The woman in the red dress sat on the concrete platform, entranced by his rehearsal.

"I'm looking forward to you playing with us." She was high on music. "Yours is a unique talent. One that we'll benefit from."

He continued through her interruption, as she promised she'd stay silent as he played. He shut his eyes and lost himself in the tune. The melody that once haunted Stanley delighted Asher. He wanted to get it right and play it solely for his enchanted dreamer.

"Why did you stop?" the woman asked.

"Something's wrong."

"It sounded fine to me. Not one bum note. Not one!"

Asher shut his eyes and played again. The wistful nature of his instrument fooled him in believing his intuition was wrong. After all, he did overthink, habitually choosing reason over intuition.

Something made him move the flute away from his lips.

"If you hinder my enjoyment one more time, I won't stay around." She huffed like the spoilt child she was. "Now play."

"No. Stanley has something to tell me. Something new has unfolded. Something he's keeping to himself."

"That upstart. Please! I don't know why you're infatuated with that nobody. Telling us we have no class. Really? A man with no life experience—"

"Shh."

"Young Ash, you are smitten. Just with the wrong person."

"Please. He's my project."

"Oh, he's more than that."

"I must go."

"Well, if you must, you must. Be a good sport. See what he wants and get over him. Damn him to uncertainty. That's his default mindset. He's been that way all through his waking life."

Asher stuffed his flute in his back pocket and left without saying goodbye. He strolled through darkness into a dream he never planned.

Stanley wandered an art gallery with a younger version of his mother. But Stanley was his own middle-aged self.

When Stanley saw Ash, his mother and the rest of the scene went hazy.

"You need to tell me something." Asher snapped his fingers, causing the fuzzy dream to fade completely.

"*I* need to tell you something?" Stanley repeated Asher's words, aware the young man was fishing.

"Yes. Something's going on in your waking life I need to know about."

"Oh."

"Anything come to mind?

"You are an inquisitive figment of my imagination, aren't you?"

"So, what should I know?"

"Franky's romancing me. That's all I can think of. Or at least, he's trying to."

"Oh."

"Don't worry. His romantic style is awkward."

A window appeared, warming the men with late afternoon sunlight. Asher ambled to Stanley and cradled his head against Stanley's chest.

Stan lifted Ash by the chin with his finger, gazing into his eyes. "You're jealous."

"Am I? Are you sure that's what I'm feeling?"

"Perhaps I shouldn't have told you."

"Oh."

"You really are jealous." Stanley pressed Asher's face back against his chest. "Mr Midnight Man, I'm not tempted by my boyfriend anymore. It's a relationship I once believed in, but it turned sour. Tragically comedic, even."

"But you're still with him."

"It's life."

"Then slip with me into eternal sleep. Please. I need you."

Silence followed. Stanley contemplated this relationship and how it could continue. Endless dreamscapes for him and Ash to share. Youthful Stan having a second chance at a charmed life. Playful sex in surreal scenarios too numerous to imagine.

"I love you, Ash."

"I love you, too, Stanley."

Asher moved away from his lover. He pulled out his flute and played the tune he'd been rehearsing. Stanley stared into the distance. Here was the lover who was considerate enough to play tunes from his past. Ash understood romance.

Chapter Nineteen

Bonding

"I'm both intrigued and delighted as to why you wanted to join us," said Adelaide to Francesco. She let him and Stanley into her apartment.

"I feel like I'm missing out on some secret club," he joked.

"No secrets here," said Stanley. "Just quality mother and son time." He stopped in his tracks. "That sounded wrong. Like we don't want you here."

"Dinky, I'm used to you putting your foot in your mouth as much as you are used to me doing the same. I know you meant nothing by it."

"Stanley will show you where to sit," said Adelaide. "We don't want you sitting at *our* designated places at the table."

She tried her best at a friendly smile, but Francesco could see her attitude. He was shown where to sit as Stanley poured three glasses of sherry.

Dinner was already at the table. Chicken was the meat of the night. Stanley knew this was mother's easiest roast to make. She'd buy a ready marinated chook from her gourmet butcher whenever she was too busy to cook, instead of making a succulent glaze for whatever red meat she was preparing. Stanley remembered she'd had an easy day. Francesco wasn't worth the effort.

"Do you ever find things in your fridge that shouldn't be there?" Francesco asked.

"Is this about the toffee apples again?" Stanley moaned, even though he knew his dream world props would eventually be discovered.

"But it's odd."

"What is?" she asked.

"There were six toffee apples in our fridge the other night. I didn't buy them. Stanley didn't buy them."

"I told him it was a figment of his imagination," said Stanley. "He dreamed them."

"No. My slippers were under our bed when I got up during the night, and I specifically put them near the bedroom door before I fell asleep."

"Why? You never do that."

"I couldn't sleep, so I moved them to prove I wasn't dreaming. They were still there in the morning. If I'd been dreaming, they'd be under the bed."

"Ghosts," said Adelaide.

"I don't believe in ghosts," Francesco replied.

"Believe in them or not, they can bring things into the material world."

"At least it's a charitable ghost," Stanley joked. "You must have upset it. Otherwise, we'd get the chance to eat them."

Francesco picked up his sherry glass. "I'm losing my mind," he said, his voice melancholy.

"At least that takes the spotlight off me and the flowers."

"Dinky, five hundred dollars' worth of flowers *is* losing your mind. So is seeing toffee apples, but at least I'm not responsible for buying them."

"Five hundred dollars' worth of flowers?" Adelaide questioned. "Did a whole family die?"

"No. I was just in a heightened frame of mind, Mother."

She knew immediately Stanley's lack of reason was because of Asher. He always lost his head in love. "But still five hundred dollars is excessive. Even for me."

"It was a flight of fancy," Stanley reasoned. "The chicken's going cold."

Francesco began carving.

★

"These martinis are wicked." Adelaide slurred each word.

"I'm glad you had the ingredients in your cabinet," Francesco replied.

"My son is going to have a sore head."

They watched him sleep on the couch.

"He won't make it to work tomorrow," said Francesco. "Hell, I don't even think he'll make it home."

"He can sleep here. In fact, you can both use the bedroom. Just put sheets on the bed before you pass out. They're in the wardrobe."

"Where will you sleep?"

"I always taxi home after our Tuesday night dinners. Well, most of the time." She leaned toward Francesco as if she had a secret. "I don't like to be here when the cleaner returns to wash up."

"That's a bit..."

"Snooty? Not really. He talks too much. If I can avoid hearing about his litter of kids and how well they're doing in their second-class education while I put on a grin and act interested, I will."

"You and Stanley could wash up after dinner. Or install a dishwasher. Lord knows you can afford it."

"But I'm doing my bit for charity by keeping my cleaner employed."

Francesco smirked, half amused, half confounded.

"You didn't join us tonight just to be social." She returned his judgemental look in her gaze. "Is this something to do with Stanley's five-hundred-dollar floral spending spree?"

"Perhaps." Francesco pointed to the balcony. "Let's talk outside."

He envied her harbour view, taking in the lights of the city behind the grey deco bridge, seeing them rendered as watercolour through his alcohol tinted vision.

"It's romantic out here," he mused. "Why don't you live here?"

"Stanley likes this place. I want it to feel neutral for him." Her lips tightened. "I didn't mean to say that."

"Neutral? Are the Tuesday dinners some sort of therapy?"

She didn't answer. She gestured to the small outdoor setting, usually more ornamental than functional. They sat.

"Adelaide, why is Stanley the way he is? You know, uncertain."

"My dear, is this really a conversation you want to have with me?"

"I feel something happened a while—"

"He's uncertain because of you."

"That's blunt."

"Well, which one of us is the expert on the subject of Stanley?"

Francesco chose his words carefully. "Adelaide, I'm not perfect, but I feel there's a young man trapped inside who is too scared to take the lead. Regardless of what you feel about me, I used to make Stanley smile, but something happened to him long before I took him for granted."

"Why do you care?"

"That's unfair. He's my man. Of course, I care."

"You don't treat him as well as you should."

He paused. "Yes, that's true. But I'm amending my ways."

"Why bother? Just let him go so he can meet someone worthy."

Francesco stared at the countless headlights darting across the bridge. Many thoughts raced through his head, all trying to numb her piercing words. And although he knew he no longer deserved Dinky's affections, he didn't want to face the looming sense of loss.

"It's pride, isn't it?" Adelaide queried. "You're not sure you want him for yourself but having him walk out on you is not the way you want to part."

"I *want* him for myself. That much I know."

"Do you? Do you really, Francesco? I may be an old woman but I'm not bloody stupid. You're a small man who believes he can have it all. No. Let me rephrase. You're a small man who believes he's *entitled* to it all."

Francesco thought back to the earlier conversation about her cleaner. *Entitled?* But he knew better than to throw that word back at her. "Adelaide, I love him."

"Do you know what love means?"

"You're the second person to ask me that."

"And probably for good reason. What does love mean to you, Franky dear?"

"It means seeing someone who makes you smile. Someone who's returned to his old self."

"That's both obscure and clichéd. I'll ask you one last time. Love! What is it?"

"It's knowing that you want to be with someone."

"Really, Francesco! Really? Well, if you want to be with someone, you can't fool around with someone else when my son's waiting for you at a restaurant."

Her picturesque view was now haunted, and as a late ferry blew its foghorn, the cityscape behind it had a collective soul. A judgemental soul peering back at him.

"I had an affair once," she said. "Someone to put a smile on my face at a time when I needed reassurance. Don't look so surprised, Francesco. I know fake astonishment when I see it."

He felt like a subordinate who disrespected the Mafia boss and was now trapped in this conversation. "Who was he?" he timidly asked.

"A younger man. A man who danced me into daydream every time we were together. Even if there was no music, he'd place his arm around me and hold my hand and pretend to waltz. We got better at it each time. Eventually, we glided across the floor. At the end of each dance, we kissed. Boy, did we kiss. But an affair is supposed to be flawless. It's about meeting someone who's perfect even though they're destined for someone else. You're just borrowing them for your own selfish need and maybe they're doing the same. But you both know there's a shelf life, and you extend it because maybe that's your last chance at happiness."

"Why are you telling me this, Adelaide?"

"You know why."

"But you don't like me."

"Just don't let it linger, Francesco. My son deserves better."

"But if you don't like me why—"

"I didn't make myself clear. For your own sake, don't let it linger. Go find the man you're supposed to be with and stop being so nondescript. That way my Stan can find the man he's supposed to be with."

Francesco swallowed hard.

"I'm not the perfect man. Hell, I don't know anyone who's perfect. But I'm too old to continue bad habits. Stanley and I were happy once. Really happy. I've been preoccupied by those happy times lately and I want them back. No, let me finish, Adelaide."

"I didn't say anything."

"But you were. I know I'm not good enough for your son, but he's been his old self lately. That self I used to nurture before I stopped and focused on my own needs." He leaned forward and checked if Stanley was still sleeping. He was. Francesco eased back into his seat. "I want that forty-three-year-old I fell in love with back, but I want to find that thirty-three-year-old and that twenty-three-year-old in the process. And I've never done that. In our seven years together, he's never totally opened up to his past."

He choked on his last word. He wiped his eyes, embarrassed at his tears. They sat in silence.

Adelaide stared into the distance. "Your problem is that you see everything from the point of view of how it relates to *you*. But do you ever notice how things relate to Stanley?"

"I think that's my problem. I'm starting to see how Stanley sees the world—"

"Way too late."

"Yeah. True."

Silence again. The ferry was now parked, and its commuters were lined up, waiting for the man at the quay to place the miniature footbridge over the water. Adelaide stood, placed her hands on the balcony railing, and watched the distant passengers.

"Ask him why he doesn't like the police," she said.

Her words were so random Francesco wasn't sure he heard them properly.

"He's mentioned police from time to time, and he freaks out over homeless people sometimes."

"But have you ever queried why he doesn't like police?"

"Of course, I have. But he never tells me."

"It's because he can't remember."

"Pardon?"

"Dig into why he fears police and you'll finally meet that younger version of Stanley you're so willing to meet."

"Wow. Really? Thanks for the advice, Adelaide."

"Advice? No, my dear. I'm giving you a test."

Chapter Twenty

Contest

"Why are we here, Ash?"

"I want to remind you that your theatre date wasn't the only time he let you down."

Stanley recognised where they were. Another Stanley was unaware of their presence as he sat watching a bad reality show by himself. He checked his phone. He put it down again when he saw no one had texted.

In time, this version of Stan wandered to the kitchen, opened the fridge, and gazed inside. Eventually, he reached for something and then changed his mind. He opened the freezer and took out a large tub of vanilla ice cream. He fished out a tablespoon and ate two mouthfuls before staring at the floor. He put the ice cream away.

He returned to the couch and channel surfed, only catching a glimpse of each image before he dismissed it. He shut his eyes, hoping to nap.

"You're never that sad when you're with me." Asher forced a smile.

"I smell fresh," Stanley noted.

"It's your cologne."

"Of course, it is. I used to wear it on special occasions."

"I like your shirt."

"It was new. I got rid of it soon after as it reminded me of this night. The night we never made it to the movies. Do I really need to relive this?"

Asher snapped his fingers. The scene disappeared. They stood in a dark room with three wooden chairs. Against the four walls, a line of small lit candles gave the space an eerie quality.

"I've known you for a while now," said Stanley. "But I've never thought you'd be this jealous."

"I'm not."

"Yes, you are. I already forgave him for not showing up at the theatre last week. You didn't need to show me the previous time he kept me waiting."

"But did you *really* forgive him?"

"Ash, I don't like your tone. Is this one of those dreams where you're going to show me how intensely you love me? Do I have to prove myself again? What's going on?"

"Calm down, darling. I'm sorry but I can't work out how you can forgive the guy who's probably got a twink of his own on the side."

Stanley breathed deeply. "You are jealous, aren't you?"

"He's playing you."

"Ash. Calm down. Make me twenty-five. Let's go on an adventure."

Asher crossed his arms. Another scene appeared.

Stanley was alone in a small restaurant. A glass of wine and a creamy pasta were positioned next to a pair of theatre tickets.

"This was the moment I decided to take my mother instead. I have you to thank for that, Ash. If you didn't show me myself as a boy, I wouldn't have treated my mother to a play."

"You're still making excuses for him."

The restaurant scene disappeared. Stanley gestured to the chairs. They sat.

"Asher, the truth is, a lot is going through my mind. Maybe I'm being lenient on Franky because I'm starting not to care. Here is where I'm truly happy, in my dreams with you."

"Then slip with me into eternal sleep."

"Believe me, I'm tempted. Living my youthful years with you is my escape."

"Then do it."

Stanley collected his thoughts. "I'm trying to make sense of my life. And I've re-examined it, thanks to you. When I'm ready to walk out on Franky I'll let you know."

"But you love me. You said so."

"I do, but how the hell do I live in a dream?"

Stanley watched the candlelight flicker on Asher's brooding face. This was one of those moments when Asher was twenty-one, believing in his grown-up self yet still with many nuances to grasp. Eventually their eyes met.

"I'm sorry," said Asher.

"Tell me something."

"Sure. What is it?"

"Why did you make us homeless and put me in the middle of a fight? When you weigh things up, that's worse than leaving me alone on a date."

"Relationships strengthen through shared experience."

"No. You were testing me. You wanted to see if I'd fight for you."

Asher grinned. "True. But look how it changed you. Look how you told the woman in red off for disrespecting her maid."

The candlelight danced on the pale-blue walls as if leaping in joy. Arms and legs in silhouette gave distraction to this strange dream.

"Are you going to perform with that group of snooty friends?"

"I don't know."

Stanley was sure he saw faces in the shadows. All friendly and all smiling. Yet he still couldn't help thinking that this dream could turn into a nightmare at any minute.

"Can I kiss you?" Asher asked.

"I'm not sure. Why are there three chairs here?"

The flames rose, causing more frenetic shapes to form in the shadows. That's when Stanley saw him. Francesco's outline boogying with the other forms. He popped out of the wall.

"What are you doing here?" Stanley asked.

"It's your dream. You tell me."

"You need to talk," Asher replied. He picked his seat up and moved it a short distance away. "Why did you leave Stanley waiting at home instead of going to the movies?"

Francesco sat. "He knows why, although I've never told him."

"What was his name?" Stanley asked.

"Kim. He came to see a production and propositioned me after the show."

"And that was more important than going on a date with the one you love?"

"I forgot about our date."

"Was Kim worth it?"

"I thought you said you forgave him!" Asher stood and then found the calm to ease himself back onto his seat.

"So, I buried the past," Stanley replied.

"Why didn't you question me about it then?" Francesco's tone was unusually kind.

"I felt too foolish to bring it up. And when you didn't say anything, I couldn't work out how to bring it up."

"I'm sorry I forgot our date."

"And you never remembered?"

"Nope."

"Why did you become self-obsessed? Was it something I did? Was it before Kim?"

"I see everything through my framework. You. What you mean to me. My job. How it gets us further in life.

Men. How addictive they are. We all see the world through our own framework."

"No, we don't. We see the world partly through our own framework, and partly through the eyes of others." Stanley wasn't sure if he felt like crying or screaming. "So, was Kim the first?"

"Yes. That's why I opened our relationship. I didn't want to cheat again."

Stan was numb.

Asher stood, knocking his seat over. "Where were you the night Stan wanted to take you to the theatre?"

"Someone didn't turn up for the evening shift, so I took it."

"I don't believe him, Stan."

"Who's the twink?" Stanley spoke calmly.

"There is no twink. No, seriously, both of you, stop giving me the evil eye. I'm not sneaking around with a twink behind Stan's back."

"Do you love me, Francesco?"

"I'm falling in love with you again, Dinky."

"Why?"

"You're different. You're your old self. Charming. Mind preoccupied, but in a good way. You breeze around our home giving it an aura."

"Ash, he sounds like you." Stanley noted how monotone his own voice was.

"No, he doesn't." Asher picked his chair from the floor and sat. "These are his words, if he had the courage to say them."

"Actually, he has said them. The other morning when he made breakfast."

"So, you know I'm falling for you again." Francesco reached for Stanley's hand. "I tried to tell you how beautiful you are. My man facing fifty is still as beautiful as the day I met him. And I said you were charming the other day, so you know these are my words, not Asher's."

Asher grunted.

"Do you suspect I'm seeing Asher?"

"How could I possibly know. He's your dream lover."

"But do you suspect?"

"The idea has crossed my mind, but I keep dismissing it. You? Cheating? No. I just believe you've found your own space."

"No, that's not true." Asher had to weigh in. "He knows he's losing you, that's why he wants you back. And you can't be the one to instigate a split. His pride won't deal with it."

"And what have you got to offer?" Francesco directed his anger at Asher. "You're three decades younger than Stan and you live in his dreams! What could you possibly give him that I can't?"

"Should I kiss you in front of Franky or should I just play it cool?" Asher asked.

"Ash, this isn't like you." Stanley's eyes darted back and forth between his suitors.

"Should I kiss you in front of Franky or should I just play it cool?"

Asher looked fierce and Stan knew better than to respond to his fragile ego.

The Midnight Man snapped his fingers. Disco balls appeared and the woman in the red dress was waltzing with the man in the jacket and bowtie. She gazed at him like a lonely widow in search of lost passion.

Asher strolled toward Stanley and offered his hand. Stanley didn't feel clumsy at being older than his dream lover. He welcomed the chance to be himself with someone who loved him. He pressed Asher's head into his chest, stroking his forehead to calm him.

Ash raised Stan's hand and waltzed. They circled the other couple. Stan took the lead. Soon, Ash smiled. His thoughts were lost in the face of a man who truly was forty-nine. Yet it didn't matter. His true love was in his arms no matter the age.

They kissed. Their dance halted as their lips lingered on something that was genuine. Two souls united. Two souls who had shared more than love.

"But are you there during his waking hours?" Francesco shouted.

"What?" Asher called back.

They were back in the candlelit room. No woman in red or man in a bowtie. Asher and Stanley slowly parted.

"But are you there during his waking hours? Can you make love in a house where you'll entertain your friends? Can you walk out of his slumber and enter our world? Can you..."

"Why did you stop?" Stanley asked.

Francesco stared at the floor. "Because no matter what I say, he can give you more." He gazed at Stanley. "Can you live in a dream?"

"It's my best option."

"Am I that bad?"

"All those times we have sex with other men, I don't think you look at me. Your mind is on your pleasure. Or seeing the other guy get off with me, as long as you're not left out. But you don't make love to me anymore. You have sex with me as long as there's others. And opening our relationship was your idea. You told me what we were doing and suddenly you're shopping for love online and I didn't feel I could say no. I wanted you to love me. I wanted you to see *The Women* and laugh with me and understand something about my childhood and why I love my mother and what she means to me and all you do is stay distant."

Francesco searched his mind for a response. "I tried to connect at breakfast."

"Why, Franky? Why?"

"I told you. I've got my old Dinky back. That's the man I want to love."

No one said anything for a while. Stanley processed. Asher strategized.

"And Franky, you can thank me for getting your old Dinky back." Asher folded his arms, smirking like a champion.

"Whatever you say, Asher, I was around for the last seven years. You've been here for a nanosecond. I know Stanley better. You think you do, but you're twenty-one. Once your idealism wanes with my man, you'll play the field. You'll make the same mistake I did with Kim and the extras in our bedroom."

Stanley had the version of Francesco he wanted. Articulate and ready to state his case for love. At this moment, real life was the best option. But he wondered if Francesco might be none the wiser about his feelings. Had the air really been cleared? Did this conversation only belong to a dream?

Chapter Twenty-One

Photos

It was Saturday and Stanley remained transfixed by the view from his balcony. He imagined Asher driving up in his sports car, parking, then calling to Stan so he could take him on an adventure in the real world. It was all he could think of the morning after his chivalrous dream.

Francesco rummaged through the top shelves of their wardrobe while standing on one of their dining chairs. "Yes!" he exclaimed and pulled out what he had been looking for. He proudly marched back with a shoe box in his hands.

"You dug out our old photos," said Stanley.

"Yeah, I'm feeling strangely nostalgic." He opened the box and let the pictures flow onto the carpet. Then he spread them to get a better look at the random images. "I've always loved this one. A Dinky self-portrait. How did you take it?"

Stanley joined Francesco on the floor. "I didn't take it. You did."

In this black and white image, Stanley gazed with affection into the lens. He picked up the photo. *A portrait of a man in love*, he thought. He imagined Francesco carefully positioning his camera, sharing serenity in this moment. That's what he once loved about owning an old-fashioned film camera. It beckoned for art to be captured. And what better art was there than new love?

"Ah, lasagne!" Francesco picked up a photo in which he was proudly displaying cheesy pasta in its baking tin. "My signature courtship dish."

"Oh my! Franky's famous dish. How could I forget? You invited me over, cooked lasagne, then told me how many other dates you cooked lasagne for. And then you admitted your sister made it because you can't cook."

"And you came over with your camera. It was the first time I knew you liked to take photographs. I was charmed. That camera is still up on the shelf next to where this shoe box sits. You should take photos again."

"It was a phase, Franky. I bought it before we started dating. I got tired of it."

"There's about sixty photos here you took when we started dating. It's a phase you should rediscover."

"You're a sentimental fool, Franky."

"And what's wrong with that?"

"It makes you sound old."

"Well, you said we should talk more." Francesco reached for one particular picture. "Look at this, Stan. A perfect portrait of Tony and Graham when you hardly knew them, yet this shows how serious Tony can be and how loving and carefree Graham is."

Stanley studied it. "They're a perfect couple, aren't they? Yin and Yang. They're not us."

"I think we fit well together."

"A little more lately than we have for a long time."

"Dinky!" Francesco looked at the photo again. "No, you're right. They fit. Just like..."

"Just like we did once."

"Like we could again." Francesco didn't wait for a response. He fished around for another specific photo.

Stanley kept holding the image of Tony and Graham. He now saw himself in their faces. Carefree Graham was the old version of Stanley which had been revived by Asher. Tony was the troubled Stanley he'd become in recent years. The troubled version fostered by Franky. *How can I trust you to save me?*

Francesco found the photo he was looking for. He passed it to Stanley.

"Ah, Kent and Sara's engagement party," Stanley noted. "They looked so happy."

"Look closely at Kent's eyes."

"Why?"

"Trust me. Just study the picture."

Stanley brought the photo to his face, noting Kent's glazed look.

"That's right! He was tripping at his own engagement."

"So were we."

"Oh yeah. We were. And then Kent put on those furry dinosaur feet and stamped around outside."

"And each time his feet hit the road those things made a growling noise."

"And Sara didn't care that he was playing. They were in love. He could have been an actual dinosaur as far as she was concerned. She still would have married him regardless."

Stanley smirked.

"What is it, Dinky?"

"Remember the museum of vacuum cleaners."

"Oh yes!" Francesco mirrored Stanley's playful grin. "We slept over and in the middle of the night I went to find blankets."

"But you came back without a blanket. You were chuckling hysterically. So much so you couldn't tell me what was funny."

"I pointed to the spare bedroom."

"You pointed to the spare bedroom, so I looked for myself."

"The museum of vacuum cleaners."

"That damn museum of vacuum cleaners! The deco upright Hoover with the fabric bag. The orange seventies bubble vacuum cleaner. The eighties brown tubular model. There were eleven vacuum cleaners! I counted them. Eleven!"

"And when we asked the next day, Dinky, Sara told us they were donated by different family members once they posted on social media that theirs was broken."

Stanley and Francesco laughed hard, and every time one of them was about to stop, their eyes met, and they started again. Stanley rolled onto his back and stared at the ceiling through watery eyes as his body convulsed with giggles. Francesco had a welcome feeling of relief over their shared mirth, and as it died down, he reached for Stanley's hand and pulled him off the carpet, gradually bringing him closer to an embrace.

As Francesco held his partner tighter, Stanley reluctantly did the same. He wasn't sure about Franky's choice to pick this moment to cuddle. To Stan, the timing was wrong.

"We were once like Tony and Graham," Francesco said.

Stanley pulled away. "I'd want to be more like Nathan and Elliot. There's a couple in love!"

"You don't think Tony and Graham are in love?"

"They're in love, but..."

"Dinky, just say it."

"Tony and Graham have worked on their relationship," Stanley replied. "Like us, they had a honeymoon period."

"But now they're established. They've built a relationship. That's what you're saying?"

"Nate and Elliot are still building theirs," Stanley continued. "But they adore each other, so they'll succeed as long as they keep communicating."

"I'm not following your point, Dinky. Where are we in comparison?"

"We're not like Tony and Graham. They fell in love and kept working on their relationship. But if you take Nate and Elliot from the point they are now, they're still in the honeymoon period. From here they'll either cement their friendship or drift apart, but I know they won't drift apart. From what I've seen, they're going to keep talking. But we didn't. We fell head over heels but took easy options. After our initial romance, we forgot to become friends."

Francesco felt the metaphorical punch to his stomach. "Maybe we could have—"

"Franky, there's no could have, would have, should have. There's only now." Stanley stared at Francesco with a distant look. "I have a memory of you and me, paint brushes in one hand and martinis in the other. You queried the name of the colour we were splashing onto the walls. We kept getting drunk and cuddled more than we renovated. And somehow, through the smell of turpentine, we made love on the carpet. That's the Nate and Elliot version of us I like to recall.

"The martinis kept flowing. Our love somehow didn't. And if I could turn back the clock and pick up from that moment we painted the walls, I would have done things differently. But there is no could have, would have, should have. There's only now."

Francesco kissed Stanley on the cheek. He wasn't sure what else to do. "I want to make you a promise, Dinky."

Stanley didn't ask. He still felt it was easier to love Asher than work on this relationship.

"No more extras in our bedroom," Franky finally said. "It's just you and me, Dink. It's just you and me."

"Are you sure, Franky?"

"Stan, I'm trying to save our relationship."

"Is this something you want to do or feel you have to?"

"It's fun."

"There's your answer. I think we've gone past the 'what we want' stage. For a long time, it's been the 'what Frank wants' stage."

"That's not true!"

But they both knew it was true. Francesco withdrew into himself, hunching slightly, then turning away. Stanley wrapped his arms around his partner from the side, making it difficult for Francesco to hug him back.

"Franky, my love, there's a version of us lost in time. We're still there painting the house while at night there's frantic passion in a bedroom with no flyscreens. I'm covered in mosquito bites by morning. You're dabbing ointment on my sores while thinking about ways to perfect your signature cocktail. And your martinis go from terrific to excellent over the years.

"And in that version are two men who hold hands every chance they get, whether it's under the table when they dine out, or simply watching television under a blanket to keep warm."

"But we don't hold hands, Dinky."

"That's my point."

Stanley stepped away. Francesco stood in silence, even though the silence crushed him. And when he went to find Stanley, he found he wasn't home.

Chapter Twenty-Two

Date

"Ah, booking for two," the waiter confirmed. "Under the name Dinky, you said?"

"Really, Franky?" Stanley shook his head. "This is what you think of when I leave you alone for a day?"

"I wasn't sure if you were coming back, and I thought it was sweet."

"Which one of you is Dinky?" the waiter asked.

"Me. I'm Dinky." His nickname sounded funny in this context. Stanley smirked.

A tacky trio of Russian musicians played and sang folk songs. Stanley was fascinated with the one handling the piano accordion. A skill unlike mastering the flute, but close to the art of piano playing. This thing breathed, gasping for the sake of each note. Then Stan focused on the meals of the other diners. He'd never had Eastern Bloc food. Piles of potatoes and fat-laden meat were stacked on each plate.

They were led to a quaint table which was pushed against a dark stained wood-panelled wall. Plastic flowers added colour. The white tablecloth was as stiff as cardboard.

The waiter pulled out their chairs and then fastidiously pushed them in as the men sat. Their napkins were whisked from the table, briefly gliding in the air as a handkerchief might when waved around by a magician, before being placed neatly in the men's laps.

"Would you like a complimentary glass of wine?" the waiter asked.

"I'd love one," said Stanley.

"Red or white?"

"White for us both," Francesco replied.

Their waiter minced away, excited to be serving a gay couple and wanting to show them they'd be well looked after by a fellow member of the velvet mafia.

"Did Graham suggest this restaurant?"

"No," Francesco replied. "One of our customers talked about it, saying it was kitsch as all hell. I thought you'd like it."

The accordion player's nimble fingers struck each key with force, filling the air with weird sounds. And although Stanley didn't understand the words the musicians sung, he imagined grassy fields and babushkas milking cows. What else would they be singing about?

"Songs of their homeland," Francesco said.

"I was thinking the same thing."

"Perhaps we should have goulash?"

"Isn't goulash Hungarian?"

"What's Russia's national dish, then?"

They studied the menus.

"They have pancakes," Stanley said.

"Too safe. Let's live a little."

"Fish loaf?"

"Could be nice. Why don't we try two different things and change plates during the meal?"

"Fish loaf and dumplings?"

The waiter returned with their wine.

"I need to ask you something, Dinky."

"Need is a very strong word."

"Don't analyse me. It's a question I need to ask out of care."

Stanley felt as relaxed as he usually was with Asher. And even with the daunting query Francesco felt compelled to ask, Stan eased back in his chair ready to listen.

"Now I'm not sure if I should ask this question." Francesco rearranged the cutlery on his grimy plate.

"You want to know if I still love you."

"No. I want to know why the police make you uncomfortable."

"Oh." Stanley sunk into his chair and then raised his head. "The truth is, I don't know."

"Sorry I asked."

"No, Franky, it's fine. I'm glad you asked." Stanley examined the colour of the wine before he clutched his glass.

"I'm not sure if it's one of those irrational fears or something I should be concerned about. I stutter while talking to people when an officer walks by. I walk in the opposite direction when one heads toward me. And I've been questioned by them a few times over minor things, but inside feelings of fear or anger or both rattled me. But why, I really don't know."

"Does it stem from childhood?"

"Not that far. My toy cop car was the thing I played with the most. That and Lego. I'd build cities and my cop car would patrol the streets. I think I wanted to be a policeman, but that boyhood dream faded."

"When exactly?"

"Like all childhood aspirations, after childhood. Boys took over. Except for boys in uniform. I've never been into them." Stanley paused to sip his wine. "Franky, why are you asking me this?"

"I'm trying to be your friend."

"In the hope..."

"What were you going to say, Dinky?"

"Would you like dessert?" The waiter startled them. He apologised profusely as they shook their heads and asked for coffee.

The accordion cheerfully sang under the skilful hands of its master, but the trio's concept of the ballad was just as cheesy as their renditions of songs from the motherland. Stanley hummed along. Francesco watched him, sensing Stan was more his own person in this moment than in all the years they'd spent together.

"Are we friends or lovers?" Francesco asked.

"I'm not sure. We make love, but does that make us lovers?"

"Maybe we're just friends who share other men?"

"That's not a maybe. That's a fact."

"Is it what you want?"

Stanley kept quiet as he didn't want to repeat the same conversation they'd had the other day, and Francesco didn't push for a response. The coffees arrived. They sipped quietly. Francesco observed aspects of the restaurant. The greasy hair of their waiter. The array of tasteless china on display at the entrance. The paint-chipped Russian dolls on the tables.

Stanley sat serenely, letting his thoughts float by while concentrating on none.

★

In bed, Francesco snuggled Stanley, and Stanley let him. There was no sex. Francesco kissed the back of Stanley's neck several times. Stanley gave his partner a peck on the lips. It acted as a full stop to Francesco's affections.

But Stanley wrapped Francesco's arm around himself, holding Frank's hand against his chest. Francesco wasn't sure how to interpret this.

A rekindling? Friendship?

Francesco conceded to take one day at a time and soon, Stanley was snoring quietly against him.

Chapter Twenty-Three

Young

Stanley sat alone at a table in the room with the crimson curtain. He ran his fingers through his hair. *Am I twenty-one?* He ran his finger between his stomach and his jeans. *Or twenty-five again?* He checked his fingers. No nail-polish.

"How are you, Dinky?"

He looked up. Francesco stood, much slimmer and with more hair. His tight ringlets were shaped into an eighties style. His shirt had dots. Lots of them.

"I'm fine, Franky."

A piano played. A female trio appeared and sang with soul. A plate of pasta came into existence in the middle of their table. One of the trio handed empty wineglasses to them, while another poured generous servings of red. They kept in tune as they wandered away.

Francesco lifted his glass. "Same date. Different generation."

They drank.

"Why are we here?" Stanley asked. "And where's Asher?"

"Can't we spend time without him?"

"So, you remember him."

"See, that's the question here, Dinky. Does he just exist in your dreams or has he invaded my subconscious? You're not sure." Francesco wore a curious smile.

"You're teasing me. And it's been a long time since you considered foreplay." Stanley matched Frank's grin.

"Hey, we're in our twenties. This is the age of less foreplay and let's just get on with it."

"Are you trying to seduce me?"

"Eat."

★

Half the pasta sat cold on its serving plate. Their wineglasses had been refilled several times.

Francesco rested his elbows on the table. "If we met in our twenties, would we have fallen in love?"

"I needed someone then. I found someone, but I wasn't ready."

"I would have cracked your veneer."

"You're sure of yourself." Stanley's laughter was partly youthful, partly wise. "Frank, for some reason we have tonight. A chance to know each other from a different point of view. And I'm enjoying this. It's clearing my head and giving me hope for our future."

"You sound like you want to ask me something."

"Yeah. Dear Franky's twentysomething self, what is love?"

"Someone who I can hold in my arms and cuddle in front of the fire."

"We live in Sydney. No one has a fireplace."

"Cuddle under the quilt."

"You're so clichéd, even at this age."

"Well, what about you, Dink? What's love mean to you?"

One of the women wanted to refill Stanley's glass, but he placed his hand over it. She wandered away.

"Having someone I can depend on and someone who can depend on me. No. Let me rephrase. Having someone who believes in me, and someone I believe in."

"That's the forty-nine-year-old version of you talking. What's the twenty-three-year-old version think?"

"Twenty-three? Is that how old I am?"

"I took a wild guess."

"Hmm. The twenty-three or twenty-one or twenty-five-year-old Stanley believes in longing. Being with someone who keeps me yearning. I go to work and yearn. I come home and yearn no more. Then I get up and do it all again."

"You're doing that now, with Asher."

"I wish I could that now, with you."

"I'm doing that now. I like my nearly fifty-year-old Dinky."

"I'm not convinced you're yearning. But what about now, seeing me across the table at an age we never met. Do you yearn?"

Francesco pondered. "You're really sexy, Stan. You have that soft yearning I noticed in that photo yesterday morning. That's one of your strengths. I've noticed it again many times while you've been remembering your dreams."

"Frank, you're addicted to anyone who yearns for you. It's just lust. Simply lust."

"You don't believe I can fall in love."

"Oh, I know you can fall in love. You fell for me seven years ago. My yearning helped." Stan chuckled. "We never fought for our relationship beyond that."

"Dink, being sad is an easy option."

"Staying silent is another."

They stared at each other, both seeing the hurt they'd just caused.

Stanley bowed his head. "If we met in our twenties, maybe we could have started like Nathan and Elliot. We would have grown together into loving older men instead of having jaded years behind us causing us to fear trying."

"We have tonight, Dinky. We have tonight."

The piano player stood and opened the curtain. "Follow this dream, because you may find eternity."

"Shall we?" Francesco asked.

Stanley shrugged. They left their wine and entered the darkness. House beats echoed. Cheers endorsed the next recorded diva. A song about deciding who to love followed. Stanley and Francesco joined their tribe. Hands in the air. Butts shaking. Feet keeping rhythm. The gays had taken the floor.

Francesco had more life than Stanley had ever seen. Stan gave a look of yearning, for he now knew the secret to keeping Franky interested. Yet he wasn't sure if he cared. His powerful weapon might never be used.

Stanley had admirers. Francesco loved that others wanted Dinky, and that Dinky didn't care. The top shelf candy was his alone. He took Stanley in his arms and whirled. He kissed him. He whirled him again.

Stanley stopped his look of yearning. He accepted twentysomething Franky. He clutched him tight, slowed him down. Danced as one in a sea of many.

A cheerful face spied them. He danced to manoeuvre closer to the couple. Stan's startled expression mirrored itself in the eyes of this man. Soon, Asher was close enough to address his lover.

"Do you like this dream?" he called to Stanley.

The couple broke apart. Others bumped into them, but their three sets of eyes were transfixed on one another.

"You really are jealous," Stanley said.

"No. Not really. I had to see for myself how you'd interact. That's why you're both here."

"But Frank isn't really here. It's my dream."

"My consciousness is," Francesco replied.

"And this dream will fade into the back of your mind like last time," Asher explained. "And no, Stanley, I'm not jealous. Otherwise, I wouldn't have given you this time with Frank."

"But why?" Stanley held Francesco's hand.

"Because I was a jerk the last time we met. So, I made it up to you. A little wine. A little pasta. A little romance. A little honesty."

Francesco recognised the tune that was playing. A favourite of his about finding the one. "You held me like you've never held me," he said.

"And you responded," Stanley replied. "Without me giving you that yearning look."

"We could've been good together."

"We *were* good together. We grew apart." Stanley reached for Asher's hand while still holding Francesco's.

The three stood as the dancing horde faded.

Stanley closed his eyes. "My dreamworld is all about love. I seem to find myself in drama and there's a large scoop of the surreal, but it's mainly about love."

"No, Stan." Asher turned to face him. "It's about the past and the future. The man in your past and the man in your future. And there's no 'better the devil you know' here. Life is about choice. There's the man who showed hope and failed, and there's me."

"Hold on!" Francesco nudged Asher aside. "You showed me love, Dinky. You must feel something. I know you do. You held me to possess me. And it felt good. Real good. We can be like Nathan and Elliot. We will be like Graham and Tony. We will be Stan and Frank. Just show me love tomorrow when we wake."

Asher lifted Stanley's hand and kissed it. "But this is the romantic Frank. He doesn't really think like this. He says what he *needs* to. He's old and self-centred. You can't change him now. But you can be forever young and show me the love you admire in Nathan and Elliot."

"But, Ash, you're old at this moment." Stanley let go of his hand. "You're not talking like a twenty-one-year-old. The young man who wants to play the flute on stage isn't here. This other version of you pops up from time to time. A darker version."

"A wiser version?"

"A version I'd like as a middle-aged man."

"Then help me get there." Asher wore a mischievous grin. "Slip with me, Stanley. Slip with me into eternal sleep."

Asher's perfect teeth were the last thing Stanley admired as his dream faded.

★

"I'm winning," Asher said.

"It's you again," Francesco replied.

A room full of tight leather and male sweat is where they found themselves. The music throbbed like an amphetamine heartbeat. Men of all ages and shapes were connected in rhythm, touch, and euphoric sensation.

To Asher's left were three guys rubbing against each other as they danced. One stroked the nipple of his nearest companion before enjoying a sloppy kiss from both his admirers.

An odd scent filled the air. Pocket-sized bottles were passed around for the men to sniff. After each hit, the older ones bopped with the energy of disco bunnies half their age.

Francesco admired Asher. "You scrub up well in a black cap and ball-hugging shorts."

"And those hairs on your chest must keep Stanley warm in winter."

"Why are you here?"

"I had to see what you dream about. I'm not surprised. I kind of like it."

"How come I'm not young like I was in Stanley's dream?"

"Because I'm not the director. This production is yours. I'm just the co-star."

Asher felt the perspiration of others splatter him. He licked the vinegary drops from his arm. The tartness startled him.

"This is what real men dream about," Francesco said. "Naked butts. Erotic manoeuvres. It's all here."

"Stanley's dreams are Disney World compared to yours."

"I suspect that's partly your fault."

Francesco guided Asher off the dancefloor and took him upstairs where several leather men were smoking cigars. The music shook the floor under their boots.

"Why are you here?" Francesco asked.

"I told you. I wanted to see what you dream about."

"Bullshit. You're here to put me in my place. Why else would you enter my dreams?"

"Why do you want Stan back?"

"You're being direct."

"Why do you want Stan back?"

"Because I want a second chance. He reminds me of his old self, and I realise that's what I want."

"Then why the leather daddies and boys?"

"Hey, I'm still a man. I have a pulse. And you've admitted you're turned on by this, Ash."

Asher nodded while picturing Stanley in leather. He then considered whether he should pop his lover into this type of dream.

"Okay, Frank, I'll say it. You know he's his old self because of me. You don't know how to keep him young. You don't know how to make him fall in love with life again. That's why he's happiest when he's with me."

"But you can't live with him in the real world."

"We've already had this conversation and you conceded I can give him more than you can. So, back off."

"But I've realised something. There's no way you can win. Stanley will meet up with you in his dreams for a while, but I know him. He's realistic at heart. He doesn't want to slip away somewhere he can't be. He'll be mine in the end."

"Or he'll end up with no one."

"That's why I'm trying."

A man in a leather vest offered Francesco a puff of his cigar. He took it and encouraged Asher to try it. Asher shook his head. Francesco puffed, blowing smoke rings in Asher's face. Asher broke the rising circles with his finger.

"What are you, Ash? A dreamtime fairy. A malevolent spirit. The Grim Reaper in the form of a boy. Someone meditating in Kathmandu who's entering Stan's mind. What are you and what are you doing here?"

"I'm a Midnight Man."

Francesco poked his finger into Asher's chest. "Then do what you need to do and let us be."

Asher grinned. He took the cigar from the man and puffed as he left Francesco's subconscious and strolled into darkness. Francesco felt he had the upper hand, but Asher knew he could give Stanley something his partner couldn't. A chance at genuine shared experiences. A chance to be like Nathan and Elliot. A chance at a relationship that didn't revolve around having sex with other men.

★

"What are you doing?"

Asher heard Matilda before he saw her.

He halted. "What do you—"

"Was that your project's partner you were talking to?" She crossed her arms and tapped her lime-green sneaker. "And why are you smoking a cigar? I've never seen you smoke."

He threw the cigar on the tiled floor. It faded away.

"Nice parlour trick, Ash. So, was that your project's partner you were talking to?"

"Yes."

"And this is his dream? It's not one you created, is it, Asher?"

"No, but the men were cute."

"And seeing them in leather was pretty cool, too, but what were you doing in someone else's dream? If Marjorie finds out, your goose is cooked!"

Asher gazed at his shoe.

"What? You can't look me in the face?" She moved closer. "Ash, I wouldn't say this if I didn't care. And that guilty 'boy next door' look is not going to save your arse if

Marjorie finds you've broken the main rule of the Midnight Men. Have you entered this man's dreams before?"

He looked up, sharing a timid grin. Matilda groaned like a parent before tidying their toddler's room. She then returned the smile.

"Yep," Asher replied. "I wanted him to see me with Stanley, so I brought him into one of our dreams a while back."

"You wicked hussy. You wanted to make him jealous." She folded her arms. "I think I would have done the same thing. Which dream was that?"

"Remember when I needed an elephant and you had to put in a special order?"

Matilda nodded. "I needed my supervisor's signature for it. Yes, I remember. You didn't trample him with it?"

"Hmm. Maybe I should have. No. That would be too alpha-male of me."

Matilda scanned their empty dreamscape for somewhere to sit. There was only darkness with a touch of muted light. She gestured to the floor. They both sat, cradling their legs with their hands around their knees.

"I don't think you're in love, Ash. I think you're obsessed."

He stood. Matilda pulled him back to the floor.

"That proves my point." She searched carefully for her next words. "I know what it's like to be infatuated with someone. I've been told to keep my obsession to myself but it's not easy."

"Who are you obsessed with?"

"Someone. My supervisor warned me not to say anything because there'd be a conflict of interest if I open my mouth and declare my love." She smirked. "No, Ash, it's not you."

"Are you sure? I've seen the way you gaze at me."

"You're cute. Of course, I'm going to gaze at you. But it's not you I think about when I'm in bed with just me and my finger."

"Ew. Gross."

"Oh, come on now. You were dribbling like a geriatric over the leather men in that guy's dream. And I'm sure you've done more than just gazed at Stanley over a romantic meal. Any mention of a girl's anatomy and you gay guys are ready to faint."

"Not many women I know talk about the kit kat shuffle."

"You don't know many women, Ash. And don't think what you do is much better. Pullin' on that thing like you're kneading dough. Watching it rise like a loaf of bread. Groaning like an ape when that ugly thing squirts. And not thinking twice when you do it in front of other men. Like a grand performance is expected."

He stared at his lap. "Hear that. Matilda thinks you're ugly."

She leaned forward and talked to his crotch. "No offence, little fella, but I'm sure you're okay looking. And don't get me wrong. I don't mind dick from time to time but..." She gazed up, whimsically.

"What's her name?"

"Who?"

"The woman you're infatuated with."

"Okay. I'll tell you but you have to swear on your dick you won't tell anyone."

"Me and my dick won't utter a word."

"Promise?"

"Promise."

Matilda lowered her voice. "Marjorie." She noted his shock. "Aren't you going to say anything?"

"You're in love with my teacher?"

She nodded.

"And that's who you kit kat shuffle over?"

She nodded again.

"Well, if you were going to masturbate over someone, Marjorie would be a good choice."

"Promise you won't tell the other Midnight Men, or Marjorie for that matter."

He raised his palm. "I swear not to tell anyone, and if my dick was at attention, he would swear, too, but I know he won't say anything." He chuckled. "Who's on top?"

"Huh?"

"When you're buttering your muffin, is she giving the orders or are you?"

"A bit of both. When you're with Stanley, who's inside who?"

"Stanley likes to top. But when I'm shucking the corn, I'm inside him."

"Shucking the corn? I think my 'kneading the dough' was better."

They chuckled.

"Look at us," Asher said. "We're reaching for the unattainable."

"But you've succeeded, in a dream sense."

"Yeah, in a dream sense." Asher looked away. "I have to go to class. Every time I look at Marjorie, I'll think of you diddling Miss Daisy."

"I wish I never told you."

"It's okay. You have something over me as well."

They stood. Matilda reached for Asher's hands and held them like they were kids in the schoolyard sharing a secret. But they sensed the anxiety within each other.

"I like you, Ash. Promise me you won't do anything stupid again."

He smiled and pulled away, and then blew her a kiss before wandering into the darkness.

Chapter Twenty-Four

Bubbles

"You haven't run a bath for years, Dinky." Francesco stood at the doorway of the bathroom as steaming water filled the tub.

"Keep an eye on it." Stanley rushed away. Soon he returned with a heart-shaped bottle. He poured its pink contents into the bath.

"You're having a bubble bath."

"No. *We're* having a bubble bath, Frank."

Francesco danced on the spot before he was aware of his own delight.

"There's one more thing we need." Stanley felt the heat of the water and adjusted the taps. "Keep an eye on it. I'll be back in a jiffy."

"Why are you doing this?" Francesco called out.

"Because I felt like it," Stanley called back. He returned with two glasses and a bottle of merlot. "Now get in the tub."

★

"I never thought you'd be romantic with me again." Francesco gazed at Stanley, imagining him in his twenties, yet couldn't understand why he was doing so. "Is this a one-night thing, Stan?"

"I hope not."

"Are you testing me?"

"No. I'm seeing if middle-aged men can start again."

"Oh shit. A hit of honesty."

"No. It might be the wine talking."

"So, that does mean you're testing me?"

"I'm testing myself as well."

"How will I know if I pass your test?"

Stanley wasn't sure how to answer. How do you tell your partner you also have a lover? That there are two men courting your affections. Or did Francesco remember Asher at odd times in his waking life?

Was Stanley supposed to love one during the day and the other in his dreams? He didn't know if he could handle slumber time adultery for the rest of his days.

"How will you know if you pass that test, Frank? I'll tell you. When there's no supporting cast in our bedroom and our lovemaking is much more satisfying. That's when you'll pass with flying colours."

"I've already promised you no supporting cast."

"And time will tell if you keep that promise."

Francesco chuckled. He caressed Stanley's feet which were near Frank's butt under the water. Stanley moaned. His sexy grin gave Francesco a sense of calm.

"We shared many bubble baths in our courting years," Francesco said.

"Usually with a joint instead of wine."

"And we'd make promises to each other."

"You promised you'd always love me, and I made the same promise back." Stanley gazed into the distance.

Francesco raised his hand, letting the water stream between his fingers. A mound of bubbles sat in his palm which he blew onto Stanley's chest.

"And we promised each other we'd always have bubble baths until the day we died." Francesco picked up more foam and playfully blew it onto Stanley's dick.

"We were idealistic back then." Stanley looked at the foam. "I'd like to think we can be again."

"Why are you with me?" Francesco asked. He blew more bubbles in hope for a lighthearted answer.

"For moments like this. I think I've been in a 'better the devil you know' state of mind. I'm changing into an 'it's up to me' kind of guy."

"What's turning you into this 'it's up to me' kind of guy?"

"Age. Reassessing my life." Stanley gathered foam and smeared it on Francesco's knees. "Let's stop talking about me. Let's talk about us. Where do we go from here?"

"Let's have date nights on the evenings I don't work."

"Dinners? Movies?" Stanley lifted his wineglass. "Theatre."

"I'm sorry I forgot. But at least you didn't break your usual Tuesday night meet-up with your mother."

"She had a great time."

"There's two movie versions of the play. I'll check if the library has them."

"Franky, trust me, those movies aren't as good the stage versions I've seen. I know. I've watched them both."

Francesco blew another wad of foam toward Stanley, making him smile.

"You know what I want for my fiftieth birthday? A yearly theatre subscription to your playhouse. I know you can get a discount, and it would be good for us to go. It's about time we actually used the perks of your job. We can have adult conversations when we dissect each play with wine and a bubble bath."

"Do you want a party for your birthday? Me and Graham have been discussing one."

"What ideas have you come up with?"

"Well, we talked about it once. We didn't really come up with ideas. But would you like one?"

"No."

"No?"

"No."

"Why not?"

"Most of the people there will be your friends." Stanley paused. "I'm going to have a big party for my fifty-first. By then I'll have a solid relationship with Tony and Graham and their friends, and a wider circle I can call my own. Franky, I'm going to do classes on my nights alone."

"What in?"

"Whatever takes my fancy. Tarot cards. Pottery. Dream analysis. Whatever allows me to meet likeminded people."

"That's why I love you, Stanley. That's why I love this version of you." Francesco looked at the towels within arm's reach. "Is your skin wrinkly? Mine is. We've spent a long time in this bath."

"What do you want to do now?"

Francesco stroked Stanley's inner thighs. Stanley closed his eyes and tilted his head back. He was aroused. He breathed in the exotic coconut scent from the bubbles. He allowed his head to get giddy from the merlot. And he welcomed Franky's foreplay.

Stanley was younger again, without his Midnight Man turning back the clock. Familiar hands were allowing him to let go of more than just his worries. They were allowing him to live in the moment. A real moment of love with Francesco, and not one he had to escape from.

Chapter Twenty-Five

School

"What's on your mind?"

Asher was deep in thought and didn't hear the question from his friend. He, like the others, waited in the unpainted cement-walled room for today's lesson to begin. He leaned in the corner flicking through his journal and deciphering the notes he took during the last tutorial.

"What's on your mind?" Declan stood in front of Asher this time, his pen tucked behind his ear and held in place by his thick head of hair. He tapped his notebook against his jaw as if keeping time for a song playing in his head.

"Sorry, Dec, did you say something?"

"Are you having a problem with your project?"

Asher didn't answer.

"Does he like you?" Declan asked.

"Yes, he likes me a lot. We're very close."

"Then why the long face?" Declan dropped his notebook. "Oh. I see. Cupid's shot his arrow."

A small person with no face opened the creaky classroom door and waved a large bell. His loose hessian robe accented his short stature as his large sleeves flapped around his wrists. He waited until the ten students waiting outside stopped chatting before he rang the bell a second time. He slipped inside before the Midnight Men strode into class single file.

Their teacher, Marjorie, leaned on the aged blackboard. Her tight latex pants squeaked as she unintentionally rubbed against its surface. She enjoyed the noise, shuddering in delight. She dragged her arm up the board toward the title of this morning's lesson. Her sleeve, also made from latex, made a new shrill sound, giving weight to the importance of the words spelt out in chalk.

The young men scurried to their usual desks and read what Marjorie was alluding to.

LOVE AND THE DEPRESSIVE PERSONALITY

"Remember, students, we covered this early in the course. Can anyone recall what we said?" She folded her arms just to savour that screech once again.

A guy with emerald-green eyes, a shade that seduced everyone at first meeting, raised his hand.

"Speak, Baxter."

"It's too risky to lure a depressive personality with flirtation, otherwise they'll fall in love with you."

"Wait. What?" Asher didn't mean to be heard.

"You weren't here for that lesson," Marjorie replied. "We hadn't recruited you yet. We did a whole morning on depressive people. You can't use the initial flirtation at dinner dream with depressives, otherwise they'll misread your signals."

"That's why we use the snooty friends dream instead," Declan explained. "It creates a bond between the Midnight Man and his project."

Everyone was gazing at Declan, except Marjorie. She faced Asher.

"You told us you *used* the snooty friends dream," she said to him. "You told us the second time you used it, it worked really well. Stanley found his mojo." She strolled between two rows of desks. "Asher proved what we mean when we say 'Repetition is important to mortals. It leads them to believe they're making connections to some deeper meaning.'" She halted next to him and leaned forward. "What's the matter?"

"Nothing." All eyes were on Asher, penetrating him like power tools.

"Didn't you read up on the lessons you missed?" Marjorie's concerned stare worried him. "You did read his file, didn't you? You knew he had a depressive demeanour. Your textbook says not to initially flirt with a depressive subject during your first meeting. They'll imprint for all the wrong reasons."

"I don't remember that part of the textbook."

"Stay back after today's class. We need to talk." She strolled to the blackboard and continued the lesson.

★

Asher stayed seated after the other students left. Stanley was his first project, and though Ash was still working out the nuances of mortal personalities, it wasn't easy while he was trying to decipher his own feelings.

"Asher." Marjorie uttered his name with an all-knowing grin. "Tell me what happened between you and Stanley after the snooty dinner dream."

"We got closer," Asher replied. "But…"

"But you didn't start with that dream." She sat at the desk in front of him. Another squeak from her jacket. Another shudder of delight.

The faceless assistant made himself busy picking up chalk, putting it back on the ledge of the blackboard, and beating the dusters with rulers. He was often dismissed from juicy teacher-student exchanges and knew if he stayed active, Marjorie wouldn't realise he was relishing every word.

Besides, who was he going to tell? He didn't have a face so even communicating with facial expressions was not an option. And he had a soft spot for Asher. The faceless assistant had helped with these classes for as long as he remembered and had an instinct for which Midnight Men wouldn't make the grade. Like him, Asher was extremely sensitive. He thought too much. This was the flaw mortals suffered from. It was no use sending them a Midnight Man with the same failings.

"Bartholomew, are you listening again?" Marjorie asked.

He fetched a bucket of water and washed the day's lesson from the blackboard.

Marjorie ran her fingers through her long jet-black hair while reading Asher. "Is Stanley in love with you?"

Asher's gentle sigh gave it away. His teacher had seen this hopeless reaction many times in her more empathic students, even if she ardently believed thoughtful pupils made the best Midnight Men.

Marjorie reached for Asher's hand. "Stanley's not in danger, is he?"

"No, he's fine. He's more than fine." Asher took in a sharp intake of breath. He sensed a tear but wiped it away before it had a chance to slither down his cheek.

"You're in love with a man who's not in love with you."

He nodded, swiftly, and sat upright in an effort to take hold of his emotions.

Marjorie rose, lifting him from his desk at the same time. "Come," she whispered.

Down the bland concrete hallway, far from the School of Midnight Men, was a bright spearmint-coloured door with a lock chained around its oversized handle.

"Do you know what's behind this door, Asher?"

He shook his head. "Declan said it's where dreams went wrong but I don't know what he means."

"It sounds like Dec doesn't know what he means either." She felt relief. This was not a place Midnight Men should know about, unless Marjorie decided to take them there. "Are you ready to see this?"

"I'm not sure. Am I?"

Bartholomew strolled toward them. He held a large brass key.

"How did he know we needed to get in?" Asher held the lock to keep it steady for the faceless assistant.

"He senses when I want to enter. He has an instinct for these things. It was part of the selection criteria when we advertised the job. A sixth sense was crucial."

After the lock tumbled to the ground, Bartholomew ran back from where he came. Before Asher could ask about the assistant's strange behaviour, Marjorie pushed the door open. They entered.

A normal street scene greeted them on the other side. Shops. Footpaths. Older model cars that seemed brand new. Honking horns. Traffic lights. The whoosh of tyres on streets dampened by rain, somewhere in the distance.

Yet, there were no people.

"Come this way." Marjorie wandered into an ice cream parlour.

Forty flavours were promoted on the huge board above the counter. The glass cabinets displaying the tubs of ice cream were so clean, Ash saw his reflection as he admired the confectionery colours of the dairy treats.

But no one was here to serve.

"I'm having a milkshake," Marjorie declared. "Would you like one?"

"Yes, please. Vanilla with maraschino cherry," he replied, noticing his favourite flavour in one of the tubs.

"We'll sit in that booth. Someone will bring them to us soon."

Asher wasn't concerned no one was there to take their order. He was a Midnight Man after all. He dealt in surreal absurdism.

The shiny red upholstery of the benches in the booth made Marjorie's latex outfit continually squelch. Even she noticed Asher smirk every time she quivered from the sound.

"We all have our kinks," she said. "Yours is falling for your project."

"I didn't mean to."

"I wish I had a new outfit every time a student said that. Ash, don't long for him. Don't wait for a sign."

"I'm not. We made love, but now..."

"You gave him the strength to find what he lost in his own relationship with what's-his-name. Marcello?"

"Francesco. And I didn't save a man from a loveless relationship. I re-established it."

"So, in a sense, you did save a man from his loveless relationship." Marjorie winked. "You did good, Ash. You did good. Stanley is happy. I know it's not what you want to hear but you steered your mortal to a better life. Good work."

"I need another project."

"No, you don't. You'll only fall for the next one on your rebound." She gazed into the distance, considering what to tell him next. "Did you ever meet Baxter? He fell hard for his first project, but he misread the signs. And I brought him here and he told me all about the man who broke his heart."

"I'm so stupid." Asher choked on his words yet still found the strength to smile.

"No, my dear young man, you're not stupid. You're a spirit with a good heart. A soul who cares for the people you bond with. Never believe anything else about yourself."

Marjorie studied his face, her maternal instincts coming to light for yet another lovelorn student.

"Ash, I have a secret, but before I tell you, you must promise what I say won't be repeated to anyone in the classroom."

He nodded mindlessly, not really in the mood to listen.

"Do you know why we brought you in at short notice?" she asked.

"I replaced someone who didn't work out."

"That's half true. You replaced someone who fell in love."

He stared at her. His interest renewed.

"Yes, Ash, you replaced Owen."

"Owen fell in love with his project?"

She grinned. "Head over heels with a woman named Kate. And yes, Ash, Kate followed Owen into eternal sleep."

"And you approved?"

"I didn't know."

"And they live here, in our realm?"

A female figure in a chequered top and skirt came to their table with their milkshakes. Asher's was full of rich red swirls inside the decorative glass and Marjorie's had varying shades of dark and milk chocolate all the way through.

"Asher, this is Kate."

Asher looked up at the woman. He swallowed the lump in his throat and then coughed it back up. He averted his eyes, but the image stayed with him. There, under her plaited hair, was a head without a face.

"Thank you, Kate."

She sauntered away.

"Asher, look at me."

He trembled.

"I only bring a student here when I need to."

"Where are we?"

"Behind the doorway to broken dreams."

Ash sat with that thought, trying to see her meaning. "That was Owen's girlfriend?"

"Once."

"And that's what happens to mortals in eternal sleep?"

"It can. Owen stopped coming to class. And he never read his textbook. But he kept seeing Kate and we didn't know. He created dreams after hours when the library was shut. Matilda was unaware he was gathering props and throwing them into the Dream Maker Machine."

More faceless people, several of them children, wandered the once empty street. Some had shopping bags. One kid carried a kite. Asher couldn't help staring, gradually grasping his teacher's point for bringing him here.

"Before you can break the rules, you need to know the rules." Marjorie took off her jacket as the squeaking sound was getting distracting. "Owen and Kate's relationship didn't work out. So here she is, without a voice. More broken than if we just let her be."

"And this could happen to Stanley?"

She nodded. "Your project has fallen back in love. Unless you know you can win him back, don't try. He's in a good place now. Let him be." She gestured to the faceless outside. "Don't subject him to this. Don't make him lose himself."

"What if Francesco breaks his heart again? Will he end up like the people here?"

Asher tasted his milkshake, waiting for Marjorie to respond. She knew he was onto something. Stanley was a depressive personality and was one broken heart away from losing himself. All Asher's work would be undone. Stan would continue through life without being heard.

"If Francesco upsets Stan again, can I save him from this place? From losing his face?"

Marjorie nodded, reluctantly. "If Francesco breaks Stan's heart, you have my permission to invite him into eternal sleep, but only if he's the most confident version of Stan who ever lived. Make sure he knows himself before you do. Promise me, Ash."

"And if I don't succeed?"

Again, Marjorie considered her reply. Before she was a teacher, she also fell for a mortal. Ruth was too tired to wash off her makeup or take off her figure-hugging white dress when Marjorie first entered her dreams. Ruth returned from a blind date that started well, but ended in disaster, so the allure of a latex-wearing sex kitten popping up in her slumber came as welcome relief.

Their first meeting was in the restaurant with the scarlet curtain. They were alone, except for their waiter who served them once, then never returned. They fell in love with each other's minds. No sex followed. The intensity of their conversation was more than satisfying.

The second date was when things got physical. Before she went to bed, Ruth meditated, burning incense and focusing on the return of her dream lover. Their rendezvous began with a light meal served inside a log cabin. And although the wood fire and the heart pattern on the king-sized bed were clichés, Ruth didn't mind. This affair was more convenient than a real-life girlfriend.

Eventually, Ruth questioned Marjorie about who she really was. She feared her sleepy-time visitor was either a demoness or a malevolent spirit. She convinced herself Marjorie had a sinister motive the moment eternal sleep was mentioned.

Ruth pulled away and contacted a psychologist. As she spoke continuously about being in love with a woman who only appeared in her dreams, her analyst saw no option but to prescribe pills. That's when Ruth truly lost her mind.

"I'm confused," Asher said. "If Francesco breaks Stan's heart, you want me to invite Stan into eternal sleep where he could lose his face? Like Kate?"

Ruth still haunted Marjorie. No one wants to be the cause of someone's insanity. In the end, only one thing saved Ruth.

Marjorie leaned into Asher's ear. "If Francesco breaks Stan's heart, find a way to heal Stan before you invite him into eternal sleep. Promise me this, Ash. You both deserve love."

Asher felt he understood.

"And if he doesn't slip with you into eternal sleep, come and see me immediately," she continued. "But make sure I'm alone."

"Why?"

"Because I have another secret to share."

Chapter Twenty-Six

Confession

Stanley scooped carrot soup with a ladle and, with precision, poured the perfect amount into the mismatched bowls each homeless person held as they made their way to his counter. Henry stood next to him, unveiling crisp garlic bread from under the silver foil. He used tongs to transfer each steaming piece to the waiting man or woman in need of a feed.

"I'm surprised you're still doing this," said Henry.

"Why?"

"No offence, but we have trouble keeping full-time working men. They don't like to volunteer after a long day in the office. They usually come in for a couple of shifts, then give up."

"I'm in a good frame of mind. I have been for a while."

"So, you have a good home life, then?"

Stanley's faraway smile said it all. He appreciated Francesco's newfound love, yet Asher's whisper of "Follow me into eternal sleep," still intrigued him. These words didn't spook him the more he thought about them. He wondered why they didn't anymore. Perhaps because Frank was finally winning. Still, he wanted to be honest with Henry.

"I have two men in my life," Stanley confessed.

"Sounds like you have too much love for one man," said a woman who wore a tattered evening dress. She dipped her finger in her soup. "You could turn up the heat on the stove, love." She accepted her garlic bread.

Henry studied Stanley.

"You don't *approve* of my two men?" Stanley asked.

"Trust me. I'm not in a position to judge."

Stanley smirked. "I'm curious."

"You can't leave a statement like that hanging in thin air," claimed a younger man in a stained white T-shirt. He waited for Henry's response.

"Pete, let it rest."

"Before I was homeless, I had lots of wild nights. Look at me. Who'd sleep with me now? Share the sordid details, Henry. I've forgotten what good sex is like."

"You never forget what good sex is like," Stanley replied. Bubbles played on his mind.

"Take your garlic bread and go," Henry said to Pete. "There are others waiting."

Pete snatched the bread and took a seat. Now it was Stanley's turn to stare at Henry.

"What?" Henry asked.

"Nothing."

"You want to know the sordid details, Stan?"

"Perhaps."

"I'll tell if you tell. Which of your two men have you known the longest?"

"My partner."

"Good. Tell me about the other one."

A short woman stood waiting for her bowl to be filled. She cleared her throat. Stanley poured the soup.

"His name's Asher."

"Oh yes. I remember you told me. How old is he?"

"Oh. He's young."

"How young?"

"Yes, how young?" asked a man with a scraggly beard.

"Young."

"Is he in his thirties?" the man queried.

"Give or take a decade."

"Your sex life sounds better than mine," Henry claimed.

"I had a younger lover once," said the man. "But she left me for an even older guy." He took his food and found a seat.

"Asher must pin you to the bed." Henry smirked.

"The sex is great. He knows where to place his assets."

"I'm too scared to ask, but does he make you feel *young*?"

"Ironically, yes."

"Why ironically?"

"It's complicated. Now tell me about your affair."

"He's a married man," Henry whispered.

"Married?" Stanley whispered back. "He has a wife?"

"No, not married married. He has a man. He's been with him for years."

"Now we're playing with fire!" said a tall thin woman with an accusing look. After she took her garlic bread, she kept eye contact with Henry while finding her seat.

"Gay men and their wandering dicks," Stanley mused.

"Pot meet kettle," Henry quipped.

"Yeah, but my main relationship hasn't been great until…"

"Until?"

"Let's just say, there's renewed hope."

"That's nice to hear. It's gotta be more stable than a twentysomething."

"I guess so. Is your guy in an unhappy relationship?"

"I think so. He doesn't talk about his partner much."

"What does he say?"

The next man in the queue didn't move after his soup bowl was filled. Henry handed him his garlic bread and pointed to a spare table.

"What does he say?" Stanley asked again.

"It's not what he says, it's the way he acts with me. Like he's searching for something he could find at home if he bothered to look. He romances me instead."

"Do you love him?"

"Stan, you know from our previous conversations I don't love him."

"But maybe things have changed?"

"I know when there's no future in something. Now, I'm waiting for him to come to the same conclusion and rekindle his own relationship. Don't look at me like that, Stan. It's happened before. I'm the compass that leads them back to shore."

"That's a healthy way to look at it. You know, Henry, I'm learning from you. I'm learning that I have to come first and that being romanced in two courts is not a bad thing, as long as I keep my head screwed on."

"It sounds like you're steering your own destiny. Are you?"

"The relationship with Asher will end, and I'm okay with that. My home life is a different matter. How I feel about it, well, I'm not sure. He's done a lot lately to win me back, and if last night is anything to go on, then I guess he's succeeding."

"You only *guess* he's succeeding?"

"It could be temporary."

"What are the stakes in each relationship?"

"My sanity with Asher."

"Just the garlic bread, love," said an old plump woman. "Your soup gives me heartburn."

"Stanley, why is your sanity at stake?" Henry asked.

"No real reason. It's just the age gap." Stanley tasted the soup. Spicy. "Henry, you said you were the compass that leads them back to shore. What did you mean?"

"I attract the ones who need to rekindle. They rekindle, then they're gone. In some ways, that's my other community service. Take the one I'm seeing now. Total seven-year itch problem. But I haven't seen him for two weeks. I don't know if he's withdrawing back to Dinky or just can't get —"

"Dinky?"

"That's what he calls his partner. I don't know Dinky's real name and I don't want to."

Stanley felt claustrophobic. Then, a sudden hyper-awareness of everything and everyone in the homeless shelter took over, which was quickly replaced with no awareness at all. His hands shook as he dropped the ladle into the soup. It sunk to the bottom of the pot.

"Do you need to sit down?" Henry asked. But he became aware of the looks the homeless were giving him. Looks that would instantly seal a guilty man's fate.

"I've got to go," Stanley whimpered. "I feel so foolish. I thought he was seeing an air-headed twink. But he was seeing a grown man."

"We need to talk."

"The exit. Where's the exit?"

"Stan, you know where the exit is."

Several pointed. Stanley ran out of the shelter. His awareness shut down. He kept running, panicking for the entire ten minutes it took him to get home.

★

Stanley stared at the bottle of sleeping tablets in his hand as he sat on the edge of his bed. Francesco wasn't home from the box office yet but there was no way Stanley wanted to be awake when he got home.

"Please be there for me, Asher," he pleaded, louder than he intended.

He looked to the dream catcher, popped a pill, and swallowed a whole glass of water.

Chapter Twenty-Seven

Fools

"I knew you'd be here tonight," said Henry. He let Francesco through his front door.

"How did you know?"

"Come on, Franky, of course you'd be here tonight."

"What do you mean?"

"Have you been home?"

"No. I came here straight after work."

"Oh." Henry headed for the fridge and grabbed the bottle of wine he needed for this conversation.

"Should I be at home? What's happened?"

Henry poured. Francesco watched. He knew Henry wouldn't answer until he was good and ready. He handed Francesco his glass of wine.

"Stan knows about us."

"You know Dinky?"

"I know Dinky."

"But—"

"He volunteers at the shelter. Wait on. How did you not know he volunteers at the shelter? Hasn't he mentioned me?"

"He hasn't mentioned you. I didn't know he volunteered."

"How—"

Francesco babbled as Henry stared at nothing in particular. Frank's reasons made no sense. He was white noise to Henry, a dramatic interlude playing in the background that was no longer entertaining.

In time, Francesco stopped. Then he muttered "I'm irrelevant."

"Franky, I haven't seen you for two weeks. And that's a good thing. Dinky has been the love of your life again and you didn't need me to fulfil whatever it was I was fulfilling." Henry swirled his wine in his glass, noticing the distorted reflection of the window sway in the liquid. "But if you didn't know the simple fact that Stan worked with me at the shelter, then I guess you may be right. You are irrelevant. So, my question to you, Franky, is what can you do now to be relevant?"

The room was quiet. Crickets chirped. A motorcycle zipped down the street.

"I'm not the evil bastard you think I am." Francesco placed his untouched wine on the coffee table. "Although everyone's been telling me I'm not worthy, but I keep telling myself I am. Or I fool myself I am. But Stanley has been my friend again. He's looked at me the way he used to when we painted our house together. Or laughed about vacuum cleaners, long story, don't ask. And I've worked damned hard on winning him back—"

"Why?"

Henry's simple question hit Francesco hard. Anger welled and then subsided. Henry held his interrogative gaze.

"Why are you mad at me?" Francesco asked.

"I'm not—"

"Yes, you are. And at this friggin' moment I'm sick of everyone judging me." Frank stood. "I need to get home."

Henry rose. "No. Sit. I'm sorry but you're right, I'm pissed off. Stanley will never talk to me again. And I'm the reason." Henry paused. "Frank, tell me. What did you think was wrong with your relationship?"

"Do I need to dredge this conversation—"

"No, *we* need to dredge this conversation up. Or maybe I need to."

"To appease your guilt?"

Henry nodded. "I need to know how I fitted into your world. It might help me understand why I thought I needed you in mine."

"Henry, I put you in this situation. I am the evil bastard. Don't look for answers now."

"I guess that makes you relevant."

Francesco chuckled. "Just for the wrong reason." He gradually sat and reached for his wine. "Can you forgive me?"

"If I have any chance to be Stanley's friend again, I have to."

"Do you forgive me?"

"Frank, what have you learned from this?"

"That I'm a selfish man. I put my own needs..."

"Why did you stop?"

"I'm not sure they were needs. Wants, yeah. But for what?"

"There had to be a reason you wanted sex with me."

"Because you're cute, Henry. Because you're sexy."

"And if it wasn't me, it would have been someone else."

Francesco rose.

"Are you going?" Henry asked.

"No. I'm pondering on my feet." He tasted his wine. "You're right, Henry. I was on the prowl. If it wasn't you, it would have been someone else. I got tired of Stanley. Of being in a relationship where I had to prop him up all the time."

"No, that's not the reason. If you instilled confidence in him in the past, then you'd still be close. You were courting me to make yourself feel better, until it got boring and you found another project. Probably other men."

Francesco felt as if his soul had stepped outside his body and was watching him, judging his motives. He looked at the floorboards. "I failed to grow up. I failed to stay relevant in my own relationship."

"But something new has happened," said Henry. "What reignited the spark?"

"That I could lose him. It's what his mother alluded to. I was worried about keeping up appearances. Of what others would say if one of us moved out. So, I stepped back into my life to see if it's where I belonged."

"Have you said this to Stan?"

"Not yet." Francesco felt a tear on his cheek. He let it find its way to his chin. "We had a bubble bath last night. We used to have them all the time. For the first time in ages, Dinky ran a bath and we climbed in. We talked and there was hope that we could start fresh. Hope that we could forget the years we drifted apart and try again."

"That was last night?"

"Yeah. Why do you ask?"

"Because you haven't been here for two weeks."

"I've been falling in love again for two weeks."

"Are you sure, because he's not a romantic whim to make you feel better about yourself."

Francesco lowered himself into the armchair and placed his half-drunk glass on the table.

"I hope so because my Dinky deserves better if I'm fooling myself." Francesco's fingertips dug into his thighs. He was unaware of his tense gesture. His own words needed to free him now. "Stanley's obsessed with a younger couple, Nate and Elliot. And rightly so. They're gaga over each other. You can see it. They amuse each other with everything each other says. They gaze and laugh and do all those things Stan and I used to do, until we didn't anymore. Until I didn't keep the romance alive after the honeymoon period. But last night, Stan let his guard down and let me in..."

"It sounds like you let *him* in."

Francesco was about to reply, until the full force of Henry's words sunk in. It was nice to hear someone praise him. "I've lost Stan." He stood. "I'm about to go home and find him gone."

"I'll vouch for you if you need me to. I'll tell Stan that I haven't seen you for two weeks until you came here to break it off. Stan needs someone to love him. If you're serious about this, then you'll need to tell him about me. Bring me up before he has a chance to."

Francesco laughed. "I did come here to break it off."

"Then tell Stanley that."

"He'll know I know that he knows if I do that. It's not the way we operate."

"But it should be. You'll never win him back if you're not honest with him now."

"I don't know."

"Do you love him?"

"Of course, I do."

"Are you sure."

"I'm sure."

"You don't want to find a random tonight to bury your sorrow in?"

"No, I won't, Henry. I won't."

"Then go home and fight for him. Because if you play him for a fool now, he'll know it. He'll know if you're worthy of loving him."

Francesco let himself out. His chaotic emotions were still sensed by Henry. He wandered back to the coffee table and stood, contemplating the label on the wine bottle. A green fairy with yesteryear charm held a bunch of grapes. It seemed to be daydreaming.

Henry wondered how the fairy approached its life. Its pixie face was too cheery to ever know drama, so Henry made a promise to himself. He, too, would take a lighter approach. Men would be allowed to fall into his arms, but he wouldn't take them seriously unless they were willing to dream with him for a better life.

He poured Francesco's remaining wine into his own glass and silently toasted his vow to the common sense he always had but rarely listened to in matters of the heart.

Stanley was sleeping soundly when Francesco entered the bedroom.

"You may have been foolish to spend five hundred dollars on flowers..." He grinned. "But I was a bigger fool for taking you for granted."

Chapter Twenty-Eight

Deal

"I know who you are." Adelaide gazed with affection at the young man in her dream. "You're Asher, my son's lover."

He extended his arm. "Am I what you imagined?"

She shook his hand. "I've seen my Stanley gaze at men. Men like you when he was the same age. But there's something about you I can't put my finger on. You're different. Your parents aren't from here."

"I'm different because I'm in your dream."

Adelaide approved of the dinner party scene she was part of. A woman in a red dress instructed her butler on the correct wine to go with their beef bourguignon. A man in a chequered jacket was smiling at Adelaide, as if she was the most bewitching temptress in the room. He reached for her hand and as she offered it, she noted her hand had no wrinkles.

Her pale dress was tight, and she hadn't seen this shape to her figure since man first walked on the moon.

She picked up her empty wineglass. Her reflection had dark hair. Not a strand of unwelcome grey.

She regarded her suitor and then grinned at Asher.

"I need a favour," he said.

"Can't you see I'm busy?" Adelaide leaned toward her admirer.

"Do you want Stanley to be with me or with Francesco?"

"Oh. I see."

She dropped her admirer's hand. It landed with a thud. She stood.

"I don't need you just yet." Asher gestured to Adelaide's seat. "But soon."

She felt her face, sliding her fingers over her flawless skin. "Can I stay like this?"

"Adelaide, that's exactly how I want you."

She beamed.

Asher leaned in. "Now, tell me about Stanley's fear of cops."

"Can I help?" Matilda called to Asher as he rushed past her desk and into the library.

"I need stuff. Lots of stuff!" He rummaged through the musical instruments.

"Do you need people to play that stuff?" She strode toward her friend.

"Yeah. I need a few people to do all sorts of stuff."

Asher inspected the violins. He picked the smallest one and ran his fingertip over a string.

"You have no idea how to play that, do you?" She handed him a bow.

"I know you don't pluck it."

"You seem scatterbrained today."

"I'm overexcited." His grin touched his ears. "You have to help me. I have an epic dream to stage."

"Hold on." Matilda went back to her desk to fetch a notebook and pencil. "What do you need?"

"A cop and a cop car."

"And a cop car? Okay. And a cop car." She wrote it down.

"Do you have a fairy tale package? You know, knights, castles, that type of thing."

"I think I know a way we can do that. Next?"

"I need a carnival again. With a Ferris wheel."

"You're taking this next level, aren't you Ash?"

He nodded.

"I mean, like do or die level, Ash."

He nodded again. "Help me, Matilda. I've got too many ideas, but at the core of this dream has to be an awakening."

"You're waking him in the middle of the dream?"

"No. I'm bringing Stanley to his demons. Well, one demon in particular."

"Oh. I see." She grabbed his hand. "Come with me."

Matilda led Asher to the front desk, let go of his hand, and wrote a note saying she'd be back in ten minutes.

Then she took his hand again and made her way to an office just past the artwork aisle.

"My supervisor's away, so we have this room to ourselves." She gestured to one of the swanky office chairs. "Sit." She sat in the other. "Tell me, why is Stanley so special?"

"Why do you ask?"

"Because you're about to do something grand. And you seem worried about failing. So, what is it about this man that's so special?"

"He deserves so much."

"That's not an answer, Ash."

Through a glass wall panel, Asher observed Baxter weaving his way around the ornaments section of the library. "Do you need to attend—?"

"No. Baxter will be here for an hour before he finds what he's looking for. Now, Ash, why have you fallen for Stanley?"

Asher grinned at Matilda, but she wasn't letting him get away without a serious chat about his feelings. When he stared blankly at her, she tapped her foot on the carpet.

"Well, okay." He smoothed back his hair. "It's like he crept under my skin."

"Crept? That sounds freaky."

"Sneaked. Found his way."

"Found his way to your heart."

Even if it was a cliché, he let the words sink in. He recalled how unsure Stanley was when they first met. How, with all the glam and glitter of their first dream,

Stan didn't feel the right to be there. Yet, that scene was taken from Stanley's past. Asher felt melancholy.

"You're reminiscing," Matilda supposed.

"Yeah. I am."

He thought about how Stanley stood up to the woman in the red dress and her friends. How he came to the aid of the maid when she was spoken down to. That's how he knew Stan was ready for the dream he was about to orchestrate.

"He's vulnerable at the moment." Asher's words hung in the air like low-hanging laundry, unable to be avoided.

"You've checked on him. Ash, you know you're not supposed to enter the mortal world and spy."

"I didn't. His mother told me." He waited for Matilda's disapproval to wane. "I want to give him an epic dream to take his mind off Franky. And to finally give him peace."

"Wow." Matilda thought about her infatuation with Marjorie and couldn't make a comparison. "Wow."

"Stanley is goofy. But a good kind of goofy. He's kind, which has been detrimental to him, but now he's found balance. He's loving. He's protective. And he's just so damn gorgeous in his twenties."

"But he's not in his twenties. And how did his mother tell you...oh, never mind. I don't need to know."

Asher was now calm. His frenzy to create the perfect dream had turned to a gentle imagining of the scene. Matilda handed the notepad and the pencil to him.

"I'm going to check on Baxter, so write down what you need and bring it to me when you're ready. But before

I go, I have to say this. Don't make promises to him you can't keep. You are a Midnight Man. You live in this realm. Stanley lives in the mortal world. You live on different plains and the only way for Stanley to be with you is for the unspeakable to happen."

Asher wondered if Matilda knew what the "unspeakable" was now that *he* finally understood. Had she known about the doorway to broken dreams all this time? Or did she have a different idea about the "unspeakable" as he once did?

Matilda clutched Asher's hand. "A Midnight Man is not supposed to fall in love. A Midnight Man helps his project to live the life they're meant to live, without fear. Let him go, Ash. Move on to your next mortal and don't fall in love." She stood and kissed him on the cheek. "But give him one hell of a final dream. Then say goodbye in a way where you'll always be in his heart."

With that, Matilda left, closing the door quietly behind her, leaving him to ponder. But Asher focused on Marjorie's words instead. He had taken Stanley this far and now his project was in pain. And Ash needed to be the person Stan turned to.

As easily as Asher could make Stanley fall for him at this moment, the best version of Stan had to comply. There was love there. Asher knew it. But before eternal sleep, Stan had to face his fears. Failure wasn't an option. He couldn't lose his face, his identity, himself, if this dream didn't succeed.

He watched his new friend tend to Baxter, trying to convince him to take an hourglass instead of a clock. Asher chuckled at her insistence, while delighted at finding a new friend.

And when this dream achieved both love and closure, Matilda would be the icing on the cake. Someone to clown around with who Stanley would also like. The cool woman in their lives with the courage to speak her mind. Someone they both needed.

Chapter Twenty-Nine

Music

Stanley heard music. He opened his eyes and saw Asher on stage with three musicians he didn't recognise. Around him were twenty or so wooden chairs with many eccentric people sitting in them. To his right was a scantily dressed woman with a snake wrapped around her as if it was part of her outfit. To his left was a young man in a fashionable suit and tie. Or at least they would have been fashionable if they weren't orange.

Behind the rows of chairs was the back of an old wooden house. This building was straight out of the pages of a medieval fairy tale, yearning for Hansel and Gretel to pay a visit and join the recital in the back garden.

Stanley had a sense of wonder he hadn't felt for a long time. He put his hands in front of his face, studied them closely, and then ran his fingers through his hair.

"I'm twenty-one," he said to himself.

Asher had been playing his flute solo. Now, two violinists and a percussionist joined the wistful tune. A woman walked onto the stage. Dark complexion. Dark sunglasses. Dark suit. She hummed the melody before singing in her lower register.

The audience swayed with the music, so Stanley also moved in time. This heightened his sense of the moment. Love, as big as the planet, made him feel that he was *as one* with the universe. Admiration followed. Then awe at what he had with Asher. Francesco didn't enter his mind. Right here was where he belonged.

He blew Asher a kiss, but Asher seemed too involved with his musicians to notice. So, Stanley turned to the gent in the orange suit and told him, "I'm in love with that flautist up there. And he loves me too."

"You're lucky to find love," he said. "Hold on to it!"

"It's funny. I used to play the flute but somehow I gave it away when I was the age I am now."

The singer's voice soared. The violins grew louder. And Asher played his instrument confidently.

The man next to Stanley tugged on his sleeve. "Why did you give up the flute so young?"

Stanley faced the man again but this time with horror. A police uniform replaced his orange attire.

"Do I know you?" Stanley asked.

"Yes."

"I don't remember you."

"Then why ask if you knew me?"

Stanley didn't know why he'd asked. He looked back to the stage.

Asher commanded his flute with each breath. He played solo with the singer, hitting notes that made the bushy hair on Stanley's head stand on end. Now the violins sung. The drums returned, beating frantically until each instrument came to an abrupt halt. The singer hit her highest peak, and in unison, the band gave the song an ending even the deaf could hear.

Everyone cheered, including Stanley who'd forgotten about the cop. And the cop was once again in his citrus-coloured suit.

The band took a bow, so Stanley stood, applauding his lover with heartfelt pride. Asher ran into his arms. They kissed. The audience cheered louder.

"We can go now," Asher said. His voice no higher than a whisper.

"Are you sure? Don't you have to play?"

"Not now that you're here."

They kissed again. "I like being twenty-one, Ash. I want to stay twenty-one with you forever." Stanley carefully scanned the crowd. "What happened to your snobby friends?"

"It was your influence. I wanted to meet nicer people. People who didn't practice the art of belittling."

A woman waving from the porch took their attention. It was Adelaide in her figure-hugging dress. Her hair as dark as coal. Stanley was pleased to see his mother young again and took Asher's hand to stroll cheerfully toward her.

"Mother, this is—"

"Asher," she said. "Yes, I know. I've never seen you smile like this, Stanley." She reached for Asher's hand. "I have to thank you for what you're doing. You made my son rediscover his youth."

"Mother, I'm not the only one who's younger."

Adelaide blushed before turning slowly like a ballerina in a music box. Fabric clung to her graceful body.

"I was a looker, once," she confessed.

"Mother, whether you're here looking younger in my dream world past, or your own age in my real life present, you'll always be the most important woman in my life."

"Your dream world. I thought I was in mine."

"You're both supposed to be here," Asher said. "In Stan's dream."

"It's a creative dream." Adelaide turned to look in all directions.

"You have a creative son," Asher replied, keeping his planning a secret. "Your influence?"

Adelaide blushed.

"Mother, you also had a younger lover when you were my age. You told me his name was Hewitt."

A figure appeared next to her. A cigarette drooped from his lips. His short dark hair glistened from styling wax. A heart-shaped tattoo peeked from under the sleeve of his white T-shirt. Then, Hewett vanished.

"Everyone in life leaves an impression," she said. "It may be a bruise. It may be a smile. It may be discomfort, like when you have a cold. And it doesn't matter how long they've been in your life, they still leave an impression."

"I see why Hewett left an impression," Stanley replied. "Good on you, Mum. He was..."

"Hot?"

"I was trying to think of a more parental word. But yes, Mother, he was hot!"

"I don't know if I left an impression—"

"Older woman, younger man. Believe me. He remembers you, wherever he is."

"Come," said Asher. "This dream sounds like it's desperate for ratings."

The Midnight Man guided them through the house. Inside, the old wooden shack was opulent beyond common sense. Knights in armour sat on floral lounges having high tea with a princess in a long scarlet gown. Kitchen hands were obsessing over the right amount of wood to place in the fire where a piglet on a spit was being roasted. A small boy sang opera while prancing around the kitchen. No one seemed to mind his high tones. In the room nearest the front door, children dressed in dark robes practised magic tricks.

"Asher, do you know these people?" Adelaide asked.

"Not personally. I know their faces but not their names."

"Where are we?" Stanley asked.

"We're back at the Carnival of Lost Souls. Stan and I have been here before."

"This is a carnival?" Adelaide scrunched her nose as she queried.

"No. It's just the name of the place." Asher led them to the front door.

"What the...?"

Stanley couldn't believe what he was seeing. There was no front yard. The doorway was the beginning of the alley where the homeless man lived.

"Asher, why are we here?" he asked.

"Because this is the moment everything changed," his mother answered.

Stanley held a flute. It wasn't Asher's. He took a closer look. It was the one he had when he was twenty-one.

"I loved playing this," he said. "Mother, why did I stop?"

"It was my fault," she replied. "I encouraged you to be independent."

"I know. That was your greatest gift to me. That and all the places you took me. But that doesn't explain why I stopped playing the flute."

"After this, I never let you out of my sight. I vowed I'd take care of you for the rest of my life."

"I'm confused."

"Who did you become after you turned twenty-one?" Asher asked.

"It was a year for city boys." Stanley laughed to himself. "City boys with too much aftershave."

"And after that?"

Someone peered back at them from the alley. It was the homeless man.

"After that I lost myself. I thought I was me, but the people around me saw me differently. I thought I played at charming, but the boys saw me as creepy. I spoke but no one heard me. I desperately wanted to find Stanley again, but I didn't know where I was hiding." He squeezed Asher's hand while looking at Adelaide. "What's down there, Mother?"

"It's where Stanley is hiding," she replied.

"I have to go alone, don't I?"

"No," Asher replied. "I'm your Midnight Man. I'm here to walk by your side."

"I love you."

"I love you too."

Chapter Thirty

Forever

Asher stepped forward, leading Stanley. Adelaide gasped, almost fainting. She covered her eyes. The lovers made their way into the dark.

"You're a brave man," said the guy who lived in the alley.

But Stanley didn't look at him. There was another figure at the far end. A figure in a police uniform, and as they came closer it was clear Stanley had met him before. He wasn't just the eccentric guy in the orange suit. His face was more familiar than that. His face was from Stanley's uncertain past.

"What kind of a pansy boy carries a flute?" he barked.

Asher was gone. The officer smashed Stanley in the face. Stan's nose pounded. Breathing was agony. Scarlet droplets coated his upper lip. Before he could get his bearing, another punch landed on his jaw, twisting his body as if he was a wet rag someone was wrenching water from. Then Stan suffered a blow to the temple. Every object in his view shimmied on its own.

"I forgot this day," said Stanley. He was standing next to Asher, unharmed, as they viewed his likeness on the ground, battered and bruised. "How did I forget?"

"Coma can cause memory loss."

"Coma?"

"Yes."

"Wow! This is when I lost myself. I played at a recital and was walking back to my car."

"I didn't know you drove."

"I stopped doing a lot of things." Stanley shivered. "My body lived my life for me, without my spirit. I spoke but people spoke over me. My tiny voice yearned to be heard, but it forgot how. I was the faceless man in the crowd."

"Keep talking, my love."

"Like I said, my spirit was gone. No one notices you when your spirit dies."

They felt heat from behind. As they turned, a bright light blinded them. Still, they moved closer. The same cop stood on the pavement with his arms crossed. Attached to his police vehicle was a globe, more radiant than any theatre spotlight, pointed straight into the rearview mirror of the car in front. In the passenger's seat of that car was a man in his early twenties wearing a rainbow T-shirt, a black beret, and a stud in his ear. He shielded his face from the overbearing light.

"Where's your spirit now, Stan?"

"It's here, Ash, and it's angry!" Stanley marched toward the cop. "Oh no you don't!" he roared.

"Who do you think you are?" the cop screamed.

"I'm your elder!"

"Elder? You're younger than I am."

"In what universe do you think humiliating this man—"

"Man? This pansy boy, you mean!"

The officer raised his baton, but Stanley couldn't stop his steady hike toward him.

"How does this give your uniform dignity?"

"Stop or I'll strike you."

"What do you mean, stop or you'll strike? I just asked you a question."

"I'll strike you!"

"And I asked how does this give your uniform dignity? But you can't answer. You can't defend your actions."

Stanley snapped his fingers. The baton burst into flames. The cop yelped like a dog who'd been kicked. He dropped his weapon to the ground.

"Kapow!" Stanley yelled. The globe blew, sending sparks flying. He headed for the guy in the car. "You can drive off now. Don't let anyone attack you for who you are. You are perfect."

He started his engine. The officer ran to his own car only to realise he was naked. Asher waved the cop's uniform in the air.

"Let's find someone who has the dignity to wear this," Stanley called. "Asher, put it on." But Asher ignored the request.

The naked policeman strutted toward Stanley, but with a snap of Stan's fingers, his cop car burst into flames.

"You're a poor excuse for a human being," Stanley shouted.

"Don't I haunt you?"

"Haunt me? You overbearing macho dickhead, I forgot all about you. You're not as significant as you thought!"

Stanley strode toward Asher, but Asher ran toward the burning police car and threw the uniform through its window. It sparked before it burned. He then returned to Stanley.

Soon they were back at the Carnival of Lost Souls. Fireworks painted the evening sky. Toffee apples, pastries, and freshly baked waffle cones were being offered by many. They passed a fortune teller's tent. Asher was keen to see the clairvoyant, but Stanley stopped for a different reason.

"What is it?" Asher asked.

"The enormity of what just happened has…"

"Caught up with you?"

"Yeah."

"Sit."

The grass was wet beneath them, but its damp was the furthest thing on Stanley's mind.

"Are you okay?" As Asher swept the hair from Stan's forehead, he felt sweat on his fingertips.

"No. I'm not okay."

Stanley rolled into a ball. Asher rubbed his back. Soon Stan was weeping in between feelings of helplessness and anger. He tried to speak but words choked him.

He whimpered instead. Then Stan felt fingernails gently stroking his back. He knew who they belonged to.

"I'm sorry, son," Adelaide said. "From here I didn't know what to do."

Asher was gone.

"I was in a coma?"

"For a while. And I went through every conceivable conversation I could have with you while you lay in hospital. 'Hey Stan, don't let this define you.' 'Hey Stan, your heart may be stone but...' What could I say? The boy I'd raised to love the world had the world strike him down. What wisdom could I share because frankly, I had none."

"Are you embarrassed by the man I became?"

"How could you think that?"

"My relationship with Franky. My lifeless job. All this with fifty a stone's throw away."

"Those aren't my reasons because I'm not embarrassed by you."

"Yeah, I know. They're mine. They're my reasons to feel embarrassed."

Stan looked as far as he could into the manic scenery that made up this dream. He roared, cursing the cop. "He took my life!"

"Yes, he did. I had a boy who laughed at circus clowns and danced every time he heard music. He was the only person who'd sing along with me to the radio. Yet after that toxic excuse for a cop ripped out your soul, I kept writing to the council to pour testosterone depleting chemicals in the water supply. But they kept telling me it was illegal."

"Mother, you were right about Frank. He was seeing someone."

"I tried to tell you. What will you do?"

"I'll stick with Asher."

"Good. Remember, you've outgrown Francesco."

"True. I have to slip into eternal sleep."

"And I'll stand by that decision. Asher is where your true heart lies."

Stanley hugged his twentysomething mother.

"Come with me." She pointed.

He looked up. A Ferris wheel was beckoning.

"Yeah, let's do this," Stanley said.

They strolled past hawkers of all types, offering wares from the sublime to the ridiculous. Alarm clocks. Insect-eating plants. Curtains. The woman who wore a snake was trying her luck at shooting metal ducks on a conveyor belt. And from afar they heard the singer from Asher's recital belting out a jazz standard.

They stepped into their carriage and closed the glass door behind them, ready to see this world from a new viewpoint.

"I'm usually scared of heights," he confessed.

Adelaide kissed her son on the cheek. Stanley touched where her lips had just been. He closed his eyes. "Mother, you never abandoned me. Please, never feel that you did."

"Thank you for saying that, my son."

He opened his eyes and saw the reflection of two twenty-one-year-old men on their carriage window. He was with Asher again.

"This is where I'm happiest. And with Mother here, it's my perfect world."

"And we can grow up together. You with confidence and me with someone to look up to. Someone who understands each age I'll become."

"I don't want to wake from this and face a man who had an affair behind my back."

Asher grinned like the devil. "But you had an affair too. I'm sure you've never mentioned me to Franky."

"But this is my dream world. You're my Midnight Man. This doesn't count. I'll be awake soon."

"Then slip with me into eternal sleep."

He kissed Stanley. Long and lingering. The dreamer felt a youthful charge. Something familiar yet not experienced for many years. His twenty-one-year-old body was responding, unrestrained and shameless. No reason to look back. He reached for Asher's crotch to feel him stiffen.

But then Stanley checked their reflection. His body was willing, but his mind was elsewhere.

"What's the matter?" Asher asked. "Everyone wishes they were twenty-one."

"But they don't have to wish. The truth is, they *were* twenty-one."

★

"Everyone goes through a mourning period, every two and a half years or so."

Stanley's mother was giving him advice in the room with the restaurant tables and the scarlet curtain. She was still youthful. He was not. Asher sat listening, seated opposite Stanley.

"That mourning period means you must give up the age you've just been, and that's not easy. We don't flow comfortably from our early twenties to our mid-twenties to our late twenties and so on and so on. We feel ourselves slow down. We know we must lose immature thought. And that's uncomfortable every two and a half years or so. We have to grow into the new version of ourselves."

"From this day forward, I will be comfortable whatever age I am," Stanley declared.

Asher reached out to him across the table.

"This is the son I set out to raise. You're your own man. Now take Asher's hand. Slip into eternal sleep. Live your life the way you were supposed to."

Adelaide faded.

"You told me you loved me." Asher knew Stan was pulling away.

"I do. You've given me so much in a way I can't explain."

"But you're not going to stay with me, are you?"

"I'm facing fifty, Ash. Every version of me still lives within me. The twenty-one-year-old. The twenty-five-year-old. Hell, even the forty-year-old. And that's why you're still beautiful to me, Asher. I never looked at you through an old man's eyes. That twenty-one-year version of me noticed you the moment you arrived in my dream world, until I remembered I was actually forty-nine. And hell, a forty-nine-year-old, or even a forty-year-old, doesn't want to relive his years."

"Even if it's with me?"

"Even if it's with you, Ash."

"I'm just glad you came under my spell, eventually."

"When I was young enough to be on the same page as you."

"To me you'll be forever young."

Stanley's weathered hands held onto Asher. From behind the breaks in the scarlet curtain, the other versions of Stanley wandered in.

He admired the forty-year-old who seemed out of step with what was going on, but Stanley knew that in a couple of years this version of him would fall in love with an Italian man. Maybe this time he'd fight to keep their love on track.

The thirty-five-year-old Stanley looked more out of place. He needed an affair to break the pattern of low self-esteem and there was someone interested back then. He should have jumped right in.

The thirty-year-old Stanley was always ready to fight back, even when it was unwarranted. He stood away from the others, yet his black nail polish still made him stand out more than his counterparts.

The twenty-five-year-old version didn't make a sound. His hands were securely placed in the pockets of his jeans.

The twenty-one-year-old strode to the table and sat next to Asher.

"I'm really the one who was in love with you from the start," he said. "And inside everyone in this room is me. My history. My growth. Who I became and how my life shaped every new version of me."

"And I don't need to give my twenty-one-year-old any more advice," old Stanley said to his younger self. "Because now I'm ready to face the fifty-year-old I'm to become." He stood. "Thank you to all the Stanleys in this room. Without you I wouldn't know me."

He took Asher's hand and raised him from his chair. They embraced with pure love. As Stanley pulled away, he wiped Asher's cheek.

"You have the world at your feet, young man. Don't squander it. Make every experience count because each will in the end. Make sure they guide you and land you safely to the other end of your life."

"I guess eternal sleep is not for you." Asher's grin was self-assured.

"No, friend. Through my dreams you gave me back my life. Now it's time for me to take charge again. Goodbye to my lover, my teacher, and my Midnight Man. Goodbye, Asher. Now, learn from me as I've learned from you."

★

Stanley inhaled, but as he sat up, he hit his head on something solid.

"Ouch!" he cried.

A crowd gasped, muffled somewhere in the darkness. Stanley raised his hand and then thumped on whatever was keeping his hand from raising further.

"He's alive," someone called.

"Open the coffin!" It was Francesco's teary voice. "Open the coffin."

"Yes, open the fucking coffin!" Adelaide screamed.

Clanging echoed inside Stanley's confined chamber. He tried to cover his ears, but the restricted space made it impossible.

"Those candle holders are useless," said another voice.

"Hold back!" yet another voice said. Something fell with a dense thud. "Put Stanley on the floor."

Stanley felt the weightless sensation he often felt in elevators before his body seesawed, causing his knees to hit the lid.

"Steady on, son!" Adelaide shrieked. "Get him out of there."

"Yes, please get him out of there." Francesco was crying.

Stanley's coffin was now level. *Thump!* The crushing sound of wood splintering frightened him. *Thump!* A tiny hole let daylight in. *Thump!* He could see something metal rising through a crack. *Thump!* Fingers reached inside and pulled at the fractured lid.

"This is no use. Hit it again."

Crash. The metal object nearly hit Stanley. Again, fingers tried to force the wood to break.

"Are you okay?" Elliot stared at Stanley through the damaged cover. "How are you alive?"

"How am I in a bloody coffin?"

"Hold back," another voice said.

It was evident the metal object was a giant cross. Elliot and the priest raised it and brought it down where Stanley's knees were. Stanley kicked. And kicked. And kicked. Fingers forced the smashed lid to break away.

Francesco moved in front of Elliot, gawking like a man seeing the dead arise.

"How did I get in here?" Stanley pushed away the last scrap of splintered wood. He sat up.

"You've been dead for three days." Adelaide stood behind Francesco. She wore a sophisticated hat Stanley knew she would have bought for this occasion.

"Is he a zombie?" Elliot asked. No one laughed.

"How did you survive in there?" Francesco asked.

"How should I know? What made you think I was dead?"

"You didn't get out of bed. I tried to wake you, but you weren't breathing. The ambulance guys said you were gone."

"Eternal sleep," Stanley murmured.

"Eternal what?" Francesco asked.

"Nothing."

"We cried for days." Adelaide removed her hat. "Days!"

Francesco knelt next to the coffin. "You're alive, Dinky. Hell, you're alive."

"Who organised my funeral?"

"We both did." Adelaide gestured at Francesco and herself.

"Do you know how you died?" Francesco asked. "Or why you're alive?" He clutched Stanley. "Hell, I don't know what I'm saying. I lost you." He stroked Stan's thinning hair and then gazed into his eyes. "Have I lost you, Dinky?"

"You almost did, Franky."

"I see." Francesco stared at Adelaide, then gazed at Stanley. "I know."

"Do you really want to talk about this now?"

Francesco nodded. He turned to the bewildered mourners. "Stan and I need to talk."

"Yes, of course," said the priest. "Everyone, move out to the yard."

"Even me?" Adelaide asked.

"Even you, mother."

"Oh." She crouched next to her son, pressing her palm to the floorboards to keep her balance. "Are you sure?"

Stanley nodded.

"Well, I'll be the next to speak to you. I have gossip that simply can't wait."

She rose and sauntered out with the others.

"Out of everything I want to talk to you about, Dinky, our relationship is the last thing on my mind. You rose from the dead after three days. And I know your mum didn't have a virgin birth."

Stanley chuckled. "I know this is the last conversation you want, but I need clarity before I face the others. Franky, give me a reason to stay."

"What can I say? Honestly, what can I say? I've dishonoured you for a very long time. So, what can I promise you, now that you know I had an affair? Friendship, perhaps. At least I hope."

"What about Henry?"

"Henry and I are over. Believe me, we are."

Stan studied his man's face for honesty. He'd never pleaded like this. Francesco's hands even came together as if in prayer.

"Who broke it off? That's a silly question. Henry did, of course."

"No, Dink. I went over to break it off and he had the same idea. He wanted to respect you as much as I do."

Stanley smirked. "I'm going to miss Henry."

"Stan, I'm sorry about my affair."

"And if I didn't know about Henry, would you still be sorry?"

"Trust me, I'm sorry, but I honestly don't know if I'd mention him if you didn't already know."

Stanley noted the echo to Francesco's words. The church was larger than he imagined would one day house his funeral. And he never imagined Elliot, Nathan, and their friends to be there. He wasn't even sure Tony and Graham would come.

"Is Henry here?"

"He nearly was. Then he had this notion that you would be staring down from heaven at him next to me in the pews. It spooked him. He sent flowers instead. Nice ones."

"Not five hundred dollars' worth?"

"No. Not five hundred dollars' worth." Francesco stopped kneeling and plonked his arse on the floor. "Do you forgive me, Dinky?"

"I'm not sure. I guess so. This is going to sound harsh but I'm not sure I care."

"Russian restaurants and bubble baths won't change your mind?"

"Maybe. Possibly. I really don't know."

"So, where do we go from here?"

"This funeral must have cost a fortune. This coffin was bloody solid. Did you buy the headstone yet?"

"You're avoiding my question."

"I know. The truth is, Franky, a lot has happened before this." Stanley gestured toward the angled roof, the metal cross next to his coffin, and finally at the general expanse of this place of worship. "Before my death, I was alive for forty-nine years. But in the past month a lot has changed."

"So, the best I can hope for is friendship?"

"I didn't say that."

"I know you, Dink. It's exactly what you're saying."

"Frank, I'm not sure what I'm saying. I have a lot to work through. A lot has changed. There's more to this story than you, me, or Henry."

"What's his name?"

"Asher."

"A lover?"

"A muse."

Francesco frowned.

"Asher's not real, but through him I re-evaluated my life."

"I don't follow. Is he a character in a television show?"

"You could say that. He had his own cinematic qualities."

Stanley studied his partner. The same self-doubt Stanley lived with most of his adult years was now a feature of Franky's psyche. A power shift had happened. One Stanley would never abuse.

"For what it's worth, Dinky, I love you. And you don't need to say it back because I know you won't mean it. But I'll wait. I'll move into the spare bedroom. I know I have a lot to prove. And I'll wait to get invited back into our bed."

Stanley was about to tell him not to change his sleeping arrangements, but something stopped him.

"Franky, I'm going to need space."

"Oh!"

"I'm not moving out. I'm just doing more with my life. I have some catching up to do."

"Okay. You're going to do that dream analysis class you spoke about. Or the tarot cards."

"Or I'll learn to play the flute."

"I'll give you space. Even on my nights off. Anything else you need me to do?"

"Yes. Can you stop calling me Dinky? It's not the pet-name of a man turning fifty."

"I mean it with affection."

"Yeah, but...no."

To Stanley's surprise, Francesco wasn't sad. And to Francesco, he had the first commandment into saving this relationship. Retiring Stanley's lovey-dovey nickname.

Stanley reached for Francesco, and Francesco shuffled closer. They hugged. Stanley held his friend tight while Francesco clutched his former lover in hope. Stan knew the story of his future no longer began in his past.

He wasn't Francesco's Dinky anymore. He wasn't anyone's anything anymore. In his arms was a man with a lot to prove, and while he considered walking out if Francesco didn't live up to his promises, he felt from this embrace that his world had options.

Stanley strolled from the church and into the front garden. A hundred questions were fired at him. Adelaide stood before her son, shouting her enquiries louder than anyone else. Stan peered past the trees and onto the street. The rubble seemed quieter as someone held his attention.

Leaning against a sports car was a youthful man, yet his age was far from young. Stanley recognised that smile. That genuine grin. The guy even had a crew cut and a boy next door look that was possessed by the man he once loved.

Adelaide snapped her fingers to gain Stan's attention. But he quickly glanced at the street again, finding the guy with the luxury car gone.

Stanley beamed. He knew he no longer needed to play the perfect son. Nor did he need to be the ideal lover. He didn't even need to be in love.

He just needed space to hear his dreams.

Acknowledgements

There are a few important people who I should thank.

First off, my beautiful husband, Warren, who has stood by me through my writing journey.

Next, Clinton, who I have to continually update with news about my writing journey, otherwise he gets annoyed.

Angus, who was there at the start of my writing journey.

Mary, who is always encouraging me through my writing journey. Thank you. I don't say it much, but it's appreciated.

Rebecca, my local partner in crime, who helps me promote the fact that I have a writing journey.

Christian, who is busy with his own writing journey.

Raevyn, who gives me a place to have a writing journey.

And Liz, who understands my writing journey.

About Kevin Klehr

Kevin lives with his husband, Warren, in their humble apartment (affectionately named Sabrina), in Australia's own "Emerald City," Sydney.

From an early age, Kevin had a passion for writing, jotting down stories and plays until it came time to confront puberty. After dealing with pimple creams and facial hair, Kevin didn't pick up a pen again until he was in his thirties.

His first novel, *Drama Queens with Love Scenes*, spawned a secondary character named Guy, an insecure gay angel who many readers argue is the star of the *Actors and Angels* series of books. Guy's popularity surprised the author.

So, with his fictional guardian angel guiding him, Kevin hopes to bring more whimsical tales of love, life and friendship to his readers.

Facebook:
www.facebook.com/DramaQueensWithLoveScenes

Twitter
@kevinklehr

Instagram
www.instagram.com/klehrkevin

YouTube
www.youtube.com/user/KevinKlehr

Website
www.kevinklehr.com

Other NineStar books by this author

Actors and Angels series
Drama Queens with Love Scenes
Drama Queens and Adult Themes
Drama Queens and Devilish Schemes

Nate and Cameron series
Nate and the New Yorker
Nate's Last Tango
The Nate and Cameron Collection

Midnight Angel
From Top to Bottom
Social Media Central
Winter Masquerade

Connect with NineStar Press

www.ninestarpress.com

www.facebook.com/ninestarpress

www.facebook.com/groups/NineStarNiche

www.twitter.com/ninestarpress

www.instagram.com/ninestarpress